Darkness of the Heart

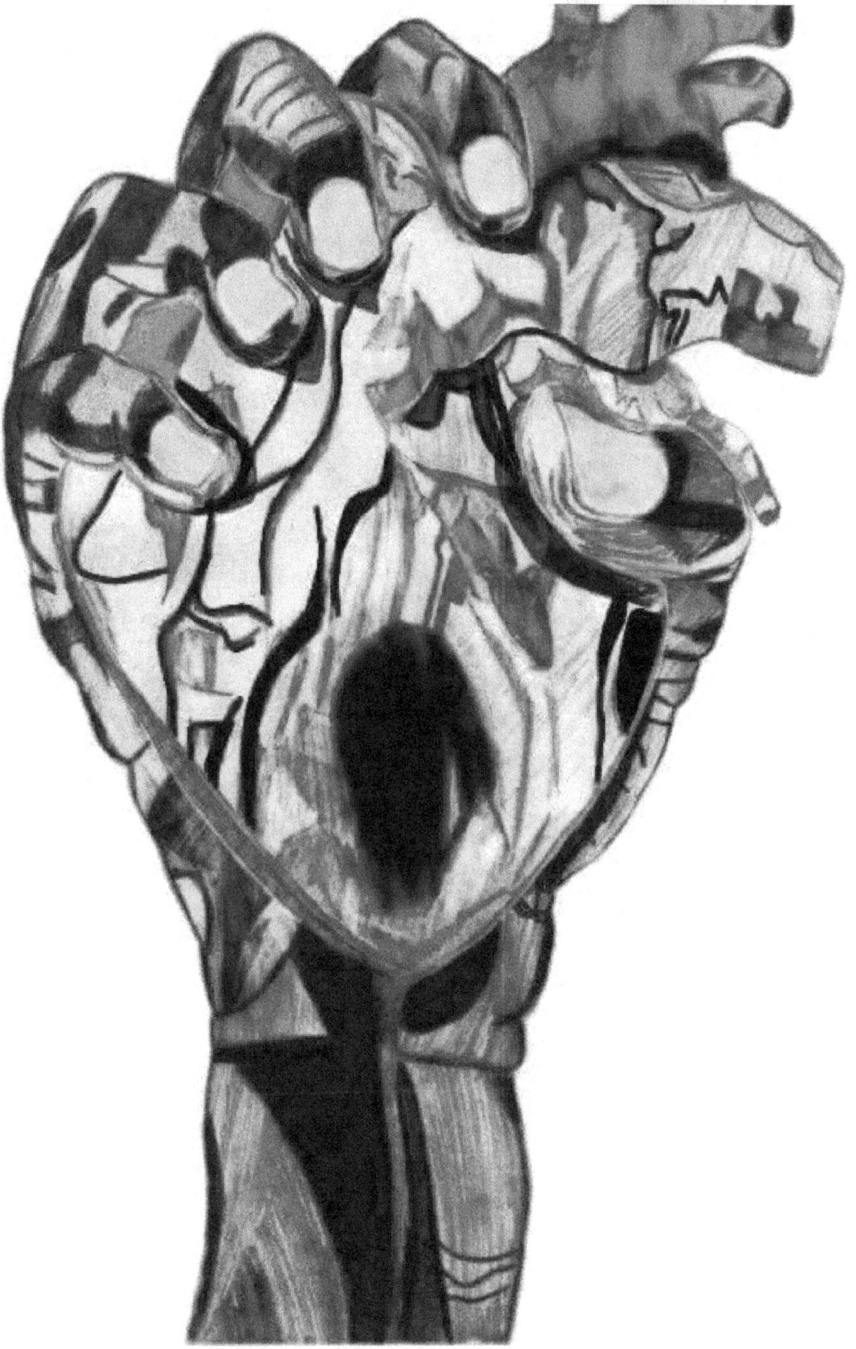

Kevin A. Dowdy

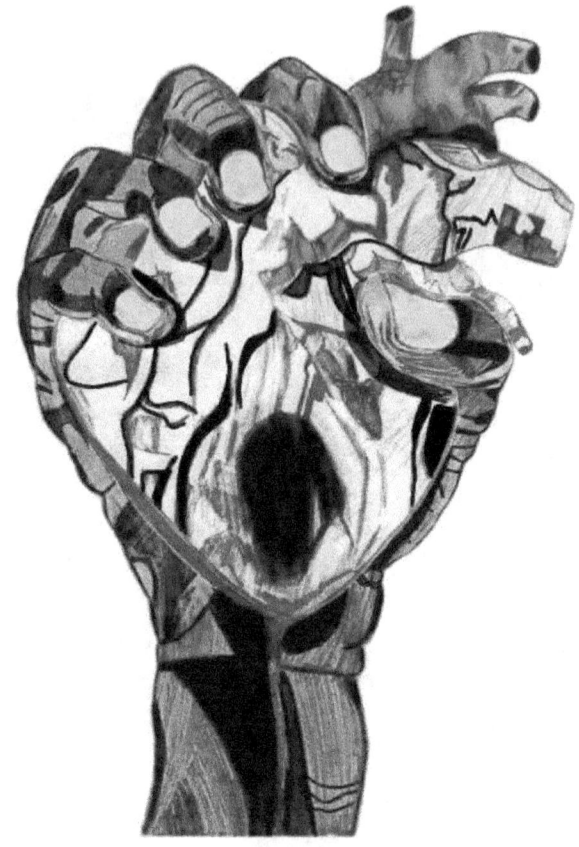

Darkness of the Heart

WRITTEN BY

Kevin A. Dowdy

Dream To Print Publishing, LLC

Windsor, Connecticut

For my family, who have stood by me through the good and bad times.

Artwork by: Dale Knight
Coloring by: Dionara Alibocas

DREAM TO Print Publishing

www.dreamtoprintpublishing.com

This book is a work of fiction. The events and characters described herein are imaginary and are not intended to refer to specific places or living persons. The opinions expressed in this manuscript are solely the opinions of the author and do not represent the opinions or thoughts of the publisher. The author has represented and warranted full ownership and/or legal rights to publish all the materials in this book.

ISBN -13: 978-0-578-49385-5

PRINTED IN AMERICA

TABLE OF CONTENTS

Chapter 1
How We Met

One night in the neighborhood, it was so quiet you could hear a pin drop. Bill lives with his mother and father; his best friend Jake lives across the street from him, and Jake's girlfriend Jay lives a couple of houses down the street.

Bill's father, an abusive drunk, comes home that night to see Bill lying on their couch watching cartoons. This angers him. He has told Bill on several occasions that he is not allowed to watch TV after 8:00 p.m. Quietly, he takes the broom that is leaning upon the door and rushes at Bill in a rage. Bill had not realized his father had come home. Then he felt that familiar blow to the back of his head, Bill jumped up screaming, his mother rushes into the living room to see what had happened to Bill. When she enters the room, she sees her husband standing over Bill, beating him with the broomstick. She rushes over and jumps between him and Bill, but the father wouldn't stop. The screams from the mother and Bill echoes out through the neighborhood. Jake sits up by his window with tears in his eyes, because this wasn't his first-time hearing Bill scream like that. Jay heard the screams, and then shakes her head, it was the summertime, and everyone in the neighborhood heard it. Bill's father stops swinging the broom because he was tired; he fell to the floor and pass out. His mother picks up Bill from the floor and takes him to the bathroom; she puts him in the shower. Both of them are black and blue when she was finished with him; his mother takes him into his room and put him to bed. His mother sits on the floor until Bill falls asleep; she stays there and cries herself to sleep.

The next morning after having breakfast with his mother, Bill asks to go outside to play with Jake. His mother tells him yes; when he was walking through the living room to go outside, his father was waking up. Bill runs through the door quickly, Jake was outside in his yard, when he saw Bill, there was sadness in his heart, but he was happy to see him.

"Bill, are you ok," Jake asked?

"Yeah, something like that." Said, Bill

"I heard you last night, why your father has to be like that." Said, Jake

"I don't want to talk about it, let's just go inside and play," said Bill

As they were going inside, Jay was running down the street, shouting at them. Jake looks around with a smile on his face, when she was close enough, she hugs Bill with tears coming out her eyes, and Bill knew that she heard what happened last night again. The three of them went inside to play games. For the next couple of weeks, Bill was going through the same thing with his father. Jake and Jay felt Bill's pain; the parents in the neighborhood begin to get concerned for Bill and his mother. The neighbors didn't want to intervene, so the beatings continue for the next couple of weeks. Bill's mother uses her body to shield him from the beatings; he was very close to his mother and felt sorry for her. Many times, he tries to stop his father from hitting his mother, but his mother would pull him back to her. Jake, Jay, and Bill became very close, after each beating the next day, Jake and Jay would be there for him. Bill had to wear long sleeves to hide all the bruises on his body; his mother never leaves the house. Because of all the bruises on her face and body, sometimes Bill would be by Jake, but his mind would be on his mother. He hated to see his mother in pain; his love for his mother was unbreakable. One day, he was leaving from Jake's house, as he was going through the door, there was a metal bat, leaning against the table next to the door, he grabbed the bat and went home. His mother was on the step waiting for him; he threw the bat in the bushes just before his house. When he sees his mother on the step, he runs to her and hugs her; they went inside. His mother put him to watch TV while she fixed dinner. When his mother went into the kitchen, Bill sneaks out of the house for the bat. He came back inside and put the bat under the chair, when his mother was finished with dinner, both of them sit at the table. Bill's mother was his world. They laugh and play at the table, and then his mother heard the front door open; she braces herself and pulls Bill close to her. The father had got fired from his job, he was in a rage, and he was drunk. He begins shouting the mother's name; Bill starts to get scared. His mother tells him to go to his room; she went out to meet him, as she enters into the living room the father hit her and she fell to the floor. Bill heard his mother scream out, he held his head trying to block out the screams, but he couldn't. When Bill couldn't block it out anymore, he left his room and went to the living room. Bill sees his father over his mother hitting her, and he runs to him screaming for his father to stop hitting his mother. The father hits him to the floor next to the couch with the bat under it, Bill reaches for the bat and gets up off the floor. He stands behind his father and begins to swing, the first hit, hits the father behind his head, the father fell to the floor. Bill stands over his father and continues swinging, the blood was splattering all over the living room. His mother was broken up. She couldn't move, the mother was spitting blood, she crawled over to Bill and held him by his leg. Bill stops and looks down at his mother; he drops the bat and holds his mother. One of the neighbors heard the screaming and ran into the house. The neighbor sees Bill on the floor holding his mother, and the father on the floor covered in blood; he quickly calls the police. A few minutes later, the police and the ambulance arrived at the house; they remove the father's body first because he was pronounced dead at the scene. The EMTs had to get the mother in the ambulance to check her; they take Bill by the police car. Jake and Jay were on the side watching; they felt sorry for Bill; the police notify the grandmother of the situation. Bill had to be rushed to the hospital, the police pass by the grandmother's house to pick her up and take her to the hospital. The mother had to go in for emergency surgery; she was bleeding in her head. The grandmother and Bill were in the waiting room; after twelve hours had passed, his mother finally came out of surgery. Bill and his grandmother had to wait for another three hours for the mother to catch herself. Before they could have gone in, the police went to talk with the mother; another hour had passed. Finally, the police came out; Bill was ready to see his mother. When he walks into the room with his grandmother, his mother had all kinds of wires and tubes coming out of her. The grandmother was crying. Bill sat at her side and held his mother's hand; the mother opens her eyes and watches him.

"My beautiful son, you are safe now." Said the mother

"Mommy are you are going to be ok; let's go home and rest." Said, Bill.

Before she could say another word, the machines started to make a lot of noise; his mother's hand drops to the side lifeless. Bill was shaking his mother and calling out to her name; the nurse and doctors came running in the room. They push the grandmother and Bill on the side, trying to bring her back to life, Bill was screaming, and his grandmother was crying. One of the nurses put them out of the room, about twenty minutes after the doctor came and watched the grandmother and shakes his head. The grandmother drops to her knees and holds Bill, "Bill was screaming and kicking, the grandmother tries to hold him, but he got away from her. He ran into the room and held his mother, shaking her telling her to wake up. The nurse and the doctor had to hold him down. They finally get him out of the room, Jake and Jay's parents drop them off, when they walk in, they see Bill's grandmother holding him on the floor. Jake and Jay run and hold him, for the next four hours, they were still on the floor; Bill didn't want to leave the hospital.

The following week before the funeral, Bill stays in his grandmother's house. Jake and Jay would come over and try to get him out of the house. Bill was missing his mother; she was his world and his protector. As the days passed, the three become very close. Jake was considered being his brother. Jay and Jake were getting closer to each other. They couldn't keep their hands off each other. The day before the funeral, Jake and Jay sleepover by Bill's to keep an eye on him, Bill was sitting by the window. As the hours pass, Jake and Jay fell asleep while Bill looks through the window. He cries through the night, missing his mother. When the sun was rising, Jake opens his eyes and realizes that Bill was still by the window.

"Hey, Bill, how you are doing?" Said, Jake

"Jake, I don't think I could survive without my mother." Said, Bill

"I am here for you, and we are brothers for life. "Said, Jake His grandmother comes to the room and tells the kids to start to get ready. Bill was in the bathroom. When Jay walks into the bathroom, Bill was walking out. Jay held him by his hand and pulled him back in the bathroom. She puts her arms around him; Bill puts his arms around her, and both of them begin to cry. Jay felt his pain and tries to be there for him. When Bill takes his arms from her, Jay watches him in his face, then she leaned in and kissed him. Bill didn't know what to do, so he kissed her back, then he realized that she and Jake were together. He pushed away and went to the room. The three of them got dressed, and they all left the house. At the church, Jay sits next to Bill. Throughout the service, Jay was rubbing Bill's leg, and he was pushing her hand away. After the service, they went to the cemetery. Bill stands by his grandmother and pulls Jake next to him. Jay walked over and held Jake's hand while watching Bill. After the pastor finishes what he had to say, they begin to lower the coffin into the ground. Bill drops to his knees and cries out for his mother. Jake came next to him and put his hand on his shoulder. Jay comes on the next side and put her hand on his shoulder. After they cover her grave. Bill stays there, crying over his mother's grave. Jake and Jay remained with him; their grandmother went to the car and waited for the kids; it was getting dark. When they reached the grandmother's house, Bill sat on the couch and didn't move from there. Jake and Jay sit with him. Everyone was giving him their condolences. As they left the house, Bill went up to his room. Jake and Jay went home. That night Bill lay in the bed and dreams about his mother. His heart was broken in half. He felt lost and didn't want to live anymore; he contemplated killing himself.

The next day, his grandmother drops him off by Jake's house to spend the day because there were three more weeks before school started. Bill was in the room with Jake playing games, and then Jay came over, and Jay and Jake were all over each other. He got up and went to the kitchen; he opens the cupboard and takes out the Clorox and was going to drink it. As he looks through the window, he sees the face of an angel in his old house, and he drops the bottle on the ground. She looked over and saw Bill standing by the window and waved at him. Bill dropped to the floor, Jake came into his kitchen and saw Bill on the floor,

"Bill you ok," said Jake

"Who is that in my old house." Said, Bill

"That's right, and you weren't here, that's Tracy she just moved in last week. She and Jay are good friends. "Said, Jake

"Really, you think Jay could introduce me to her," said Bill Jake calls out to Jay. When she comes into the kitchen, Jake begins to explain to her about Tracy. She didn't like the idea of introducing Bill to Tracy. She got up from her chair and went over to Tracy. Bill was watching through the window. Every time Jay pointed over to him, he hid. Jake looked through the window and saw that Jay was coming. He begins to laugh and tells Bill that they were coming over. His heart starts to race; Jay and Tracy walk through the door. Bill was in a daze. He couldn't believe how beautiful she looked up close. Jay introduces her to Bill; Tracy stretches out her hand to him. Bill held her hand when their hands connected, the electricity that went through Bill's body made his mind explode. Tracy was talking to him, but he couldn't hear anything. Jake walks up to him and hits him behind his head, and then he said hi to Tracy. Jay was upset at how Bill was all mesmerized over Tracy; Jake had to hold her by her hand and pull her out of the kitchen. The time was getting close to start school, and Bill and Tracy were getting closer. Jay wanted to be around them, but Jake always pulled her away. Finally, the day for school was tomorrow, Bill was excited. Being around Tracy reminded him of his mother, the way she smiled, the way how she held his hand and rubbed the back of his head, when he looked at her face, he saw his mother. Bill knew she was the one for him, his soul mate. That night before school, he did not sleep. When the grandmother opens his bedroom door, Bill was already dressed. He sits by the table while his grandmother prepares breakfast. When he finished his breakfast, he ran through the door and waited for the bus to come. The bus went around and picked up Jake, Jay, and Tracy, Tracy sits by Bill and Jake, and Jay sits behind them. The bus arrived at the school. Bill grabs Tracy's bag and walks with her off the bus, with a glow on his face that lights up the hallway. By the time the classes were set up for the kids, Bill, Tracy, Jake, and Jay were in the same class. Bill made sure that he was sitting next to Tracy, for the next couple of weeks, Bill was very happy. One day on the bus to school, Bill switches seats with Jay and sits next to Jake, he asks Jake to go to the back of the bus with him.

"Jake, I am going to ask Tracy to be with her. What do you think," Bill asked?

"Yes, that's great, you guys look good together," said Jake

"I am going to ask her lunchtime when we are outside," said Bill

During the class, Bill was waiting for the bell to ring to go to lunch. When the bell rings, all the kids run outside. The four of them went on the far side of the playground to be away from the rest of the kids. Bill's nerves were a wreck; he wanted to ask her to be his girlfriend, but he was scared that Tracy would have told him no. Jake and Jay were on the other side of the tree, kissing each other; Bill takes a deep breath. Also, asks Tracy to be his girlfriend, Tracy didn't say anything right away. Jake and Jay watch from behind the tree to see what Tracy would say. The bell had just rung for the kids to come into their class. Bill looks around, and kids were running back to class. He begins to walk away when Tracy holds his hand and kisses him and said yes. Bill was on top of the world, Jake was laughing, and Jay was just smiling. Tracy and Bill held hands as they were walking back to class. When school was finished, and they were going on the bus, Bill was delighted. On the bus going home, Bill and Tracy sit next to each other, and Jake and Jay were seated right behind them. It was the sweetest ride home for Bill; He held her hand all the way home.

For the next couple of weeks, they couldn't keep Tracy and Bill apart, and the back of the bus was their seat. One day at school, it was almost time for them to go outside and play when the bell rang. Bill quickly rushed over by Tracy and held her hand to go out. Tracy didn't want to hold his hand. However, she did, they reach outside by the tree, Bill leans over to kiss Tracy, but she puts her hand up and stops him.

Bill was a little confused and took a step back; Tracy looks at him,

"Bill look I like somebody else," said Tracy

"But why, I thought that we had something special," said Bill

"Yes, we did, but that was last week," said Tracy

Tracy walks away and then went to the other boy. He was standing on the other side of the playground. Jake and Jay begin to laugh at him; Bill stands there with tears in his eyes and starts crying by the tree. Everyone who was on the playground heard crying. Everyone looked around and saw it was Bill and began to laugh that made Bill cry even more. When the bell rang, all the kids went back to class. The teacher came outside to get Bill. He didn't want to go to class, his heart was broken, and everyone was making fun of him. The teacher walks Bill into the classroom, and everyone was laughing. The teacher tells everyone to be quiet, and she takes him to his seat. Jake and Jay were feeling bad for him, and they had a laugh at him too, Jake tries to get his attention in class. However, Bill was not talking to anyone. He looks up and sees Tracy watching the next boy. He had a lot of pain in his chest; he couldn't stand to see Tracy liking another boy. That whole week during recess, Bill would be on the swing watching Tracy play with her new boyfriend. Some of the kids would point their fingers at him and laugh.

Jake and Jay would be by the tree, feeling sorry for Bill. One day that week, Bill couldn't take it anymore, he decided that after school, he would follow Tracy's boyfriend home. When everyone was loading the buses, he notices that Tracy's boyfriend didn't get on the bus. Bill hides behind the tree in front of the school. Jake was looking for Bill on the bus. Jake thought that he had missed the bus. As the bus was driving away, he saw Bill standing behind the tree. He figures that Bill didn't want to ride the bus because everyone was still teasing about last week.

Bill saw Tracy's boyfriend walking away from school, so he begins to follow him. The boyfriend lived in the neighborhood close to the school; Bill begins to walk back home; All he thought was how he could get the boyfriend out of the way. Tomorrow is Saturday; Bill decided that he would go and talk with the boy to leave Tracy alone. The following morning, Bill was thinking of an excuse to tell his mother to go and look for Tracy's boyfriend. Bill tells his mother he is going by his friend's house down the road for the day to help him with his homework. He goes through the door. Bill tells his grandmother bye and left. Bill had packed his bag with some stuff to eat and drink. It was a long walk to the next neighborhood. Bill finally arrived, and he heard laughing and screaming. When he looks over by the playground, many kids are playing baseball. When he takes a good look, Tracy's boyfriend was playing baseball with the kids too. He went up in the woods overlooking the playground and watched from there. Bill sat there for hours watching and waiting to talk with Tracy's boyfriend; No one saw him standing there. One of the boys hit the ball into the woods; the ball landed next to Bill. He ran to the tree behind him and hid. Tracy's boyfriend shouted that he would go for the ball, and Bill was nervous. Tracy's boyfriend was coming. He went running into the woods for the ball, he was looking around and couldn't find the ball, everyone was shouting to hurry up. When he finally saw the ball, it was over by a tree where Bill was hiding as he bends down to pick up the ball.

Bill steps back so he couldn't see him and steps on a stick. The boyfriend heard a noise and looked behind him. He did not see anybody; when he looks in front of him, he saw Bill standing there. Bill panics and picks up the stick and pushes it in his neck. The blood was gushing all over, He drops to his knees, but he could not scream. Bill couldn't believe what just happened. Tracy's boyfriend was on his back, trying to breathe. Bill stands there didn't know what to do, him holding Tracy's hand flashes in Bill's head. Bill stands over him, watching him fighting for his life, and Bill kneels on his chest and watches him straight in his eyes until he stops moving. Just to be on the safe side, Bill picks up a rock and bashes his head. Bill walks away with a smile on his face.

The boys at the playground were waiting for Tracy's boyfriend to come out of the woods. They begin to shout out to him, and there was no answer, it was getting late, and they were getting worried. The rest of the boys decided to go into the woods to look for Tracy's boyfriend. As they enter into the woods, they were calling out to him; it started to get dark. Finally, one of the boys saw his shoe sticking out from behind a tree. The boy shouted that he found him; everyone else came running towards where the boy was standing. They all stood there afraid to approach Tracy's boyfriend because they were calling out to him, and he wasn't answering. One of the boys was saying that he was dead, everyone was scared, and one of them picks up a stick. The boy walks slowly towards him, he pokes his foot with the stick, as everyone was behind him. They jump back, and they encourage the boy to go and look around the tree. As he looks around the trees, he starts screaming. The rest of the boys came running around the tree to see what was wrong; there was blood on the ground. Tracy's boyfriend laid there with the stick, sticking through his neck, and his eyes were open; all of the boys jump back. They begin to run down towards the playground, some of the boys' mothers were there waiting on them; some of the parents were scared. Seeing their kids running out of the woods screaming, they quickly run to their kids to find out what was wrong. A couple of the kids drop to their knees and start to throw up. One of the boys tells his mother what he saw in the woods. The mother let the other parents know what was going on in the woods; they quickly call the police.

The boy, who was Tracy's boyfriend's best friend, tells his mother who it was in the woods. The mother holds her head and begins to cry; he asks if he could go and get his best friend's mother at her house. The mother tells him to go ahead. The boy went running to the house; he had tears in his eyes. When he arrived at the house, he stands by the door for a while, trying to catch his breath and to tell her. The boy heard the mother in the kitchen; he takes a deep breath and burst through the door. The mother threw the pot she had in her hand up in the air when she turned around and saw who it was. She begins to fuss at him; she notices that he had tears in his eyes; the mother felt something was wrong with her son. The boy explained to his mother what happened to her son in the woods. She passed out on the kitchen floor, and then the father came into the kitchen. The boy explains to the father what had happened; he quickly picks up his wife off the floor and puts her in the car. They rush over to the woods, by the time they got there, the news cameras were already there. The father jumps out of the car and begins to run up into the woods, but the police stop him. The father was kicking and screaming, trying to reach his son. When the mother opens her eyes and sees all the flashing lights and news cameras, she fainted again. The father drops to his knees, calling out his son's name; everyone who was around beginning to cry. The paramedic was working on the mother in the car, trying to revive her when they brought the body out of the woods. They brought the father to identify the body; the father starts screaming.

"Not my son, not my son oh God not my son," screams the father

Bill was at home in his room, lying on his bed looking at the ceiling. He was going through mix feelings. Didn't know if to feel happy or sad, he heard the TV turn on downstairs. He knew the news was coming on soon because his grandparents watch the news around this time. Bill hurries downstairs to watch the news with his grandparents; however, he sits in the kitchen listening to it. After the news came on, Bill heard his grandmother shout, "Oh my God." He begins to laugh; his grandmother calls out to him. Bill walks into the living room, trying to hide his smile; she asks him if he knew the boy and if he goes to his school. Bill takes a good look at the boy and turns to his grandmother. Also, he tells her he didn't know the boy, as he was walking up the stairs, he was laughing. Bill lies on his bed, and five minutes after he heard the phone ringing, his grandmother shouts out to him to come for the phone. He was confused, who would be calling him now, and then he thought it was Tracy. Bill rushes down the stairs to the phone; he trips running to answer the phone. His grandmother and grandfather watched him and shook their heads. Bill picks up the phone. It was Jake on the phone. Bill was disappointed, and Jake was telling him about the news. He didn't care to hear about Tracy's boyfriend; he quickly chases Jake off the phone and goes back to his room. Bill couldn't sleep that night; he patiently waited for the morning to come so that he could talk with Tracy. With her boyfriend out of the way, he knows Tracy would come back to him. As the morning came, Bill was the first one by the table waiting for his breakfast. His grandmother put his breakfast on the table. Bill eats so fast; his grandmother was surprised, as he runs through the door; he was the first kid by the bus stop. He sits there waiting for the bus; the other kids were showing up one by one. Jake was the last one to reach the bus stop; he was trying to talk to Bill about the news.

Nevertheless, Bill was not paying attention to him. When the bus arrived, Bill rushes into the bus leaving Jake talking. Jake had to run on the bus to meet him; the bus was coming up to where Tracy is picked up. There were three kids outside waiting on the bus, but Tracy wasn't one of them. Bill was upset because she was not there. Jake mentioned to him that Tracy was messed up about the news last night. Bill turns to him and wonders how Jake had known this; Jake explains that he had spoken with Tracy last night. He didn't like the idea that Jake was talking with Tracy. The bus reaches the school. Bill got up and walks away from Jake; Jake is confused. He saw Jay standing outside, waiting on him. Jay tells Bill hi, but he walks past her, Jake held her hand, and they went the other way. When Bill was walking to his class, the police was in the office talking with the principal, when Bill saw them, he hurries to his class. During his class time, Bill couldn't wait for the bell to ring, so he could go and get Tracy back into his life. The bell had finally rung, Bill was the first one out of the class running to the playground. He went to the tree where they usually meet and waited for her, Jake and Jay saw him by the tree and went someplace else to stay. It was getting close to the time to go back to class; Bill realizes that Tracy is not in school today. Bill begins to walk back to his class before the bell rings, and then he heard a girl crying that sounded like Tracy by the swings. He looked over and saw a group standing around a girl. He focuses on the girl; it was Tracy. Bill calls out to her, just as he suspected, Tracy, runs right into his arms. He had a big smile on his face; Jake was standing at the back of Tracy and saw the smile on his face. It didn't look or feel right the way Bill was smiling. It crosses his mind for a second that Bill had something to do with Tracy's boyfriend's death.

Chapter 2
College Life

Throughout all the years in school, junior high school, and High school, the group of friends stick together. Bill and Tracy went through many breaks up, but at the end of the day, Tracy would end back up with Bill. The relationship was very unusual, but Bill had loved her to death, Jake thought it was an unhealthy relationship. It was prom night, Bill and Tracy dressed in the same color and style outfit, Jake and Jay weren't on good grounds. Jay was getting tired of Jake, and she was jealous of Tracy, Jay liked Bill for a long time and now was seeing him treating Tracy like a queen. She didn't like it; Jay felt that she should have been the one with Bill that night Bill went to the bathroom, and Jay saw him walk away from Tracy. Then she follows him, Jake sees her walking away from him, but he didn't care, he went and talk to some girls on the side. Bill was washing his hands and getting ready to leave the bathroom when he heard the bathroom door open. He dries his hands, about to walk out of the bathroom, when the person grabs his hand when he looks up, it was Jay.

"Jay, what the hell you are doing." Said, Bill

"Don't act like you don't know, I wanted you for a long time, and that bitch stole you from me," said Jay

"What the hell, listen to me, Jake is like a brother to me, and I can't do my boy like that. Furthermore, I am in love with Tracy, you are the one that introduced her to me," said Bill

"I don't love him, there I said it, it's been a long time I stopped loving him, right now I want you in me," said Jay

Jay pushes him against the wall, begins to kiss him, Bill tries to push her away, but he didn't want to hurt her. She put a hand in his pants and grabs his dick; Bill stops putting up a fight. Jay went on her knees and put it in her mouth. He grabs onto the wall, Tracy starts to get worried because Bill was gone for a long time, so she went to the bathroom to look for him. When she was walking down the hallway to the bathroom, Tracy begins to hear moaning coming from the bathroom. When she reaches to the boy's bathroom, she puts her ear to the door. She heard Bill's voice saying, "Jay, stop, Jay stop." Tracy covers her mouth, Bill's sensation to cum was strong, Tracy flashes in his mind, and he pushes Jay off of him. He pulled up his pants up and went through the door. Tracy hides around the corner. Jay sits on the floor and laughs to herself. She gets up and washes her face and mouth and walks out of the bathroom. When Bill reaches back to the dance floor, he sees Jake over in the corner, talking with some girls.

"Excuse me, Jake, you saw Tracy," said Bill

"I saw her walk to the bathroom area about five minutes ago," said Jake

Bill's heart sinks, he wonders if Tracy heard them in the bathroom, then he finally sees Tracy walk out to the dance floor. He runs to her and hugs her, and she hugs him back. Tracy was upset, but she takes a couple of deep breaths and plays it off. Bill was trying to feel her out, but things had seemed normal, so he continues to enjoy his night with Tracy. A little while after, Jay walks out and sees Jake talking with the girls over in the corner. She walks over there and begins to cuss at Jake. Bill looks over and Jay blows him a kiss, he quickly takes Tracy on the other side of the dance floor. However, Tracy stood by him no matter what. At the end of their senior year in high school, they got accepted to the same college. Bill was very excited that he would be with Tracy, but she didn't feel the same way because of Jay. As the time was getting close for them to attend college, a couple of weeks before they left, Jake and Jay went through a bad break up. Bill didn't care what had happened between Jake and Jay, once it didn't affect him and Tracy's relationship.

The first day on campus, Bill and Jake went to get the room at the dorms, and Tracy and Jay did the same thing. After getting their rooms, the group went to register for their classes. It was an exhausting day for everyone. By the time they finished, it was very late, they all went to dinner close to the campus to grab a bite to eat. After they finished the dinner, Bill was rushing to go back to the room so that he could freshen up, and he could sneak over by Tracy's. When Bill and Jake reach back to the room, Bill jumps into the shower; Jake shakes his head, knowing that he wanted to go by Tracy. He was happy, because Jake had the room to himself, and it seems like it would be like this every night. As Tracy crawls into bed, there was a knock at the door; her roommate answered the door. She shouts to Tracy; it was Bill by the door. Tracy takes a deep breath and goes to him; he was all smiling. Tracy tries to explain to him that she was a little tired, but he kept insisting on coming in to lie down with her. She gives in and lets him in. Bill was very excited; Tracy lies on the bed when Bill lays next to her. Tracy turns her back to him. Bill puts his arms around her, and she didn't feel comfortable. Her feelings for Bill had changed over the years; many times, she tries to tell him but was always scared of how he would react. Even when they're having sex, she was just going with the flow, but she felt nasty about it. Bill was the happiest man on earth; he had the girl of his dreams and the best relationship. It was getting very late; Tracy turns around and tells Bill he had to go. He got up and kissed her, then went through the door. When Tracy closes the door, she wipes her mouth off. Her roommate watches her and laughs, Tracy begs her not to say anything to him. The next day while Tracy was in her first class of the day, she couldn't concentrate in class. She was trying to think of a way to tell Bill it was over between them. During the breaks between the classes, Jake saw Tracy in the library looking very depressed

"Hi girl, why you look like that, like your whole world, is coming down on you," asked Jake

"Hi Jake, you are so right, I don't know what to do," said Tracy

"Talk to me, maybe I can help you," said Jake

"I don't know about that, because it is about your friend," said Tracy.

"What did he do now?" said Jake.

"He didn't do anything; it's just that I don't love him anymore. I want to go out and test the sea," said Tracy.

"Tracy, all I could tell you, let him know how you feel," said Jake.

"You know you are right, I will talk to him tonight," said Tracy

Tracy got up and hugged Jake, at that moment, Bill walked through the library door and saw Jake and Tracy. Jake kisses Tracy on the cheek and then walks away. As Jake was walking away, he saw Bill standing by the door. Then Jake calls out to him, Tracy looks around and saw him too, so she puts up her hand to wave at him. She calls out to him to come over, and Bill walks slowly over to her, feeling very funny. Tracy's heart was beating fast when Bill reached the table; Jake walks over to him and puts his hand on his shoulder. Bill did not like the idea of Jake talking to Tracy, and putting his arms around her, but he brushed it off that minute. Jake felt the cold shoulder from Bill, so he walked off and left them. As Jake was walking away, Bill was so upset; he begins to have a flashback of the boy he had killed in elementary school. Tracy put her hand on his face, and then he shakes it off, and focuses on Tracy,

"Bill what you are doing tonight?" asked Tracy

"Well baby I just have a study group tonight, but I could cancel that to be with you," said Bill

"No Bill after will be good," said Tracy

"Okay baby," said Bill

Bill gets up, leans over, and kisses Tracy on her lips, but Tracy did not kiss back. Bill notices that but he did not say anything about it, Tracy was anxious because she knew he was going to take it hard. She remembers what happened in fourth grade. She worries that he might have a breakdown. However, she couldn't go on like this any longer, as she watches the time, her heart races faster and faster. After the study group, Bill rushes back to his room, he freshens up and takes a box out of his bag. Jake was curious about it was, so he asks him what it was, Bill opens the box and shows Jake. He couldn't believe it. Bill had an engagement ring. Bill explains how long he had it, waiting for the right time. Jake wanted to tell him what Tracy wanted to talk to him about, but he didn't. Bill left the room with a big smile on his face, couldn't wait to be with Tracy. Jake tries calling Tracy to warn her about the ring Bill had, but she wasn't picking up. He knew that it wasn't going to end well with Bill, Jake grabs his jacket and rushes out of the door, trying to beat Bill to Tracy. By the time Jake reaches to Tracy's building, Bill already beat him there; he watches as Bill walks into the building. Bill reaches by the door for Tracy's room; he stands there and takes a deep breath before he knocks on the door. Tracy opens the door and tells him to come in; she didn't greet him with a kiss as usual. He was puzzled for a second, she holds his hand and walks him to the bed, and Tracy sits him on the bed. As Tracy was going to say something, Bill put his finger over her mouth and got down on one knee. Tracy tried to stop him, but he would not let her. Bill reaches into his back pocket and pulls out the ring, Tracy starts to cry, at that same time. Tracy's roommate walked into the room and saw Bill on his one knee; she begins screaming. The roommate calls out to the rest of the girls in the hallway; Bill was very nervous with all the girls in the room.

"Tracy, all that we have been through and you still being at my side, would you be my wife?" Asked Bill

The room gets very quiet, the girls and the roommate were by the door waiting for an answer. Tracy didn't know what to do, so she takes a deep breath and looks at Bill in his eyes. The girls by door move in closer to hear Tracy's answer,

"Bill I am so, so, so sorry, but I can't," said Tracy

"But Tracy, I thought that we had something good, did I do something wrong or say something wrong, just tell me I'll change!"

"Bill it's not you, it's me I just don't love you anymore," said Tracy

Bill's eyes fill up with tears, he begs and begs Tracy not to do this to him, he tells her he will change. Tracy was feeling very sad for him, but she couldn't go on living a lie with Bill. His nose was running; the tears from his eyes were flowing like a river. Tracy tries to pick him up from the floor, but Bill didn't want to move, and the girls in the room started to laugh. Jake was outside, and he could hear the girls laughing, he knew that Tracy had broken it off with him. He shakes his head, feeling sorry for Bill, Jake knew he would go crazy over this, and he went back to the room to wait until Bill came to the room. Tracy gets upset with the girls because they were laughing so loud. Tracy got up and chased the girls out of the room. Bill finally got up and leaned against the bed. Bill begins to wipe his face-off, he had a sharp pain in his chest, and he starts to take a deep breath, to see if the pain would go away, Tracy finally got all the girls out of the room and then closed the door. Bill starts begging her to give him another chance; Tracy repeats herself repeatedly that it was over between them. Bill bowed his head, got up, and walks to the door, as he was turning the doorknob.

"Bill hope we could be friends," said Tracy

"I don't think so," said Bill

When Bill left the room, he slammed the door, letting Tracy know that he was very upset. As he walks down the hallway, all the girls were against the wall with their heads down. As Bill leaves the building and closes the door behind him, the girls were laughing so loud that he heard them as he was walking away. Tracy reaches for her cell phone and realizes that Jake was calling her, so she calls him back. Before Tracy could say anything, Jake explains why he was calling, Tracy tells him her phone was in her bag. She tells him what happened; Jake could only imagine how Bill was feeling right now, he tells Tracy to hold on. Jake heard Bill coming down the hallway, and he quickly tells Tracy he would call in the morning. As Bill walks into the room, he slams the door so hard it shakes the whole room; Jake jumps up and asks him what the problem is.

"Dude what's your problem, you knock me out of my bed," said Jake

"It's none of your business," said Bill

Bill lay in his bed and turns his back to Jake; Jake knew that Bill was hurting; he lay in his bed watching Bill. Throughout the night, Bill was twisting and turning in his bed; he was mumbling some stuff. Jake couldn't understand what he was saying, but Bill was dreaming about the little boy that he killed. He had a lot of anger in him. Jake knew this wouldn't turn out to be good. When the sun finally came up. Jake got up and got ready for his first class. Bill was still in his bed, and Jake looked over at him and shook his head. He walks over to Bill to try to wake him up; Bill pushes Jake off; Jake looks at him funny and leaves the room. For the next couple of days, Bill didn't want to leave the room, all he heard was the girls laughing at him.

Moreover, Tracy screaming no, he was devastated; his whole reason to attend college was because of Tracy; he didn't have any more interest in staying in college. Bill looks out the window like his whole world was coming down. One day Jake came back to the room, Bill was still in his bed, and the room was very dark. Jake turns on the light, and sits by him on the bed,

"Would you turn off the fucking light," said Bill

"No, you need to listen to me, look Tracy isn't the only girl in the world," said Jake

"So, she told you," asked Bill

"No man it's all over the campus, you need to leave that girl alone and move on," said Jake

"She was the only girl I ever loved, and she was my first, how can I move on from that, you tell me," said Bill

"Hey man I don't know what else I could tell you," said Jake

Jake tried for the whole night to talk some sense into Bill and reminded him that Tracy wasn't the only girl in the world. Bill did not say a word, just was listening to what Jake was saying, he couldn't get that image out of his head when Jake was hugging Tracy in the library. The sun was coming up soon, Jake was tired, and so he went to bed. Bill was full of so much anger that he couldn't sleep the night; he had time to think things through. He knows that he still had a chance with Tracy; Bill decided that he would stay and try to get back with Tracy.

Jake left the room before Bill; he was felt sorry for him and afraid that he won't snap out of this one. Bill got up from the bed and went in the shower; he cleans himself up and then left the room. As he was walking up to the building to go to his first class, Bill saw Tracy under the tree across from the building. She wasn't alone, Tracy was leaning on the tree, and the young man was over her. The young man had his hand on her waist and passing his other hand through her hair. Bill felt light-headed, and his eyes turn bloodshot red with anger. They were laughing, and Bill thought she was telling him about the other night in her room. Tracy looked up and saw Bill standing by the building, and she waves to him, but Bill looks away from her and goes into the building. Tracy tells the person she was coming back.

"Hey Tracy, who is that?" asked the guy

"That's my ex, nothing to worry about, "said Tracy

Tracy runs down Bill and stops him in the hallway; He couldn't watch her in her face. Tracy puts her hand on his chin and turns his face to her, Bill was distraught, and Tracy realizes that.

"Hi Bill, how you doing? I didn't see you for a couple of days," said Tracy

"How would you think I would be, after you broke my heart?" said Bill

"Bill doesn't start, why can't we be friends," said Tracy

"Don't start you say, how the fuck you expect me to feel, and just brush everything we had under a rug. By the way who the hell is that?" said Bill

"He is just a friend and none of your damn business!" said Tracy

"So how fucking long this was going on?" said Bill.

Tracy got so angry with Bill, and slaps him, Bill watches her in surprise, and then walks off. Tracy watches him as he was walking away. After Bill was gone, Tracy felt bad. Bill sits in his class by the window and watches the person under the tree, and Bill marks his face. Bill was trying to concentrate on his work, but it was hard for him because he was getting a flashback of the boy that he killed in elementary school.

Every time he would look out the window, the person would be there talking with all kinds of girls. Then the thought crossed his mind; he needed to kill the person as he did with the boy years ago. After his third class, Bill walks the campus looking for the person who was talking to Tracy earlier. While he was walking through the campus, Bill saw a flyer on a tree, about a frat party they are going to have by one of the frat houses. He knew for sure that the person who was talking to Tracy was going to be there. It was the first one they were going to have, Bill stopped looking for the person and went to his next class. At the end of the class, Bill went back to the room to rest for a little bit; Jake was already in the room. He was going to one of the frat houses.

"How was your first day back on campus, and you know there is a frat party later on tonight. Will you go," said Jake

"It was ok today, but Nah that is not for me Jake," said Bill

"Well your loss, don't wait up for me," said Jake.

As it begins to get dark, Jake finishes his classwork and goes to freshen up to get ready for the party later. Bill lay in the bed, reading a book waiting for Jake to leave the room. When Jake was finally ready, he asks Bill one more time if he was coming and reminded him that it was going to have many girls there. Bill tells him, no, and then Jake left the room. Bill waited for a while, then got up, and went through the window. He hides behind some bushes; the frat house was just up the road from his building. It had seemed like everybody was at the party. Many people were at the front of the house, so Bill went around the back; There was a bucket on the ground next to one of the windows. Bill stands on the bucket and peeps through the window; it was crazy inside. There were many types of alcohol and drugs, the room was full of smoke, and you couldn't make out who was in there. It was the perfect setting for Bill; he just needed to get inside without anybody recognizing him. Before he steps off the bucket, he saw the person he wanted; he was staggering through the crowd of people. Then the person fell on the table where there was cocaine and sticks his face in it. He sniffs so hard that he had a brain freeze. Bill smiles because everything is working according to his plan. Bill saw the person stagger up the stairs, he jumps off the bucket and went by the back door, when he pulled on the door, it was open. He slips right in; no one saw him. There was one of the beer hats on the chair by the back door; he puts it on and goes up the stairs. Once he got upstairs, he was looking through all the rooms and did not see him. Then he heard coughing coming from the bathroom. Bill walks quietly over by the bathroom and turns the knob for the bathroom door. It was unlocked, so he slowly turns the knob and opens the door. When Bill got inside the bathroom, he locks the door. The person had his hand on the wall leaning over the toilet pissing. There was a bag sticking out of the person's pocket; it looked like cocaine. Just as the person was finishing, Bill rushes the person, pushes him against the wall, reaches for the bag out of his back pocket, and pulls the bag out. Bill shoves the whole bag of cocaine into his mouth and then covers his mouth with his other hand. The person had no choice but to swallow the cocaine. When Bill felt that he had swallowed everything, Bill releases the person. He drops to the ground and starts shaking up and foaming from his mouth. Bill stands over him and looks at him until the person stops moving. Bill had a smile on his face, and then he heard someone knocking on the door. Bill opens the bathroom window, and he quickly climbs through it. Bill jumps behind the bushes under the window. He stays there for a little while and then runs back to his room. When he reaches back to the room, his adrenalin was pumping; it felt so good to him. He knows after this, Tracy will come back to him.

Back at the party, the line was building up by the bathroom; the people begin to get impatient. One of the boys who was in the back of the line walks to the front and kicks the door down; he saw the person lying on the ground. When he went over and kicked his foot lightly, the person's head drops to the side, and foam was coming out of his mouth. He stumbled out of the bathroom and fell to the floor. Everybody else looks into the bathroom, the girls begin to scream, and everybody runs downstairs. One of the campus securities was passing by, and one of the students stops him and explains what was going on. The security quickly notifies the police; within five minutes, the police and the ambulance were there. The paramedics quickly went upstairs to check the person in the bathroom; they pronounce him dead at the scene. The paramedics let the police know that the person had died of an overdose, and then the cops chased everyone from the house.

Chapter 3
The Feelings

Jake left running from the party; he couldn't wait to tell Bill what had happened at the party. He rushes into the room, and Bill was in his bed, he jumps up when Jake rushes into the room. Before Jake could have said something, he had to catch his breath; Jake sits on the chair next to his desk. He begins to explain what happened to someone at the party. Bill acts as if he was surprised. Bill asks him if they know who it was that died at the party. Jake tells him that security had chased everyone downstairs before he could find out who it was. Bill was laughing in his head while Jake continues telling the story. It was getting late, so Bill tells Jake he was tired and needed to rest. Jake got up and went to the bathroom to freshen up. By the time he came out of the bathroom, Bill had the sheet over his head. Jake had gone into his bed to sleep. Bill was waiting for the morning to come so, he could go to Tracy's so that he could have her back in his life.

When Jake got up to get ready for his classes, he looks over by Bill, and notice he was already gone. He was happy for Bill that he was back on track with his classes; Jake gets ready for his classes, and then left the room. Bill was all around the campus looking for Tracy when he passed the library, he saw her with a male talking. Tracy didn't look sad or was crying, and she had her hands all over the guy. Bill was by the door watching how Tracy was all over him. Bill was confused, Tracy should have been in tears, and looking for him, but it was the opposite. For ten minutes, Bill stands by the door, watching her with the guy. Tracy puts her arms around him. Bill couldn't take it anymore, he pushes the door for the library so hard, that it almost breaks, he walks over to Tracy.

"Tracy can I talk to you," said Bill

"Bill don't you see I am talking with someone right now," said Tracy

"But I need to talk to you right now," said Bill

Bill grabs her by her hand and proceeds to pull her away from the table; Tracy knocks his hands off her. The guy, who was at the table with Tracy, stands up, holding Tracy's hand,

and pulls her to him. Bill looks in his face and walks off. He turns to Tracy and asked her who that was,

"Tracy who was that asshole" ask the guy

"That asshole was my ex-boyfriend," said Tracy

"Your ex he looks like he is not over you as yet," said the boy

"We just friends," said, Tracy

The boy laughs aloud; he never heard of an ex being a friend, Tracy was feeling bad after Bill had walked away. However, she blows it off, she sits there and continues to talk with the guy, and he couldn't stop laughing. Bill was walking through the campus thinking, where did he go wrong, because the last time she came back to him. He stands in front of his building, thinking hard, and when it came to him. The guy reaches to Tracy before him, and that is why she didn't come back to him. Bill begins to think, how he can get rid of this boy so that he could get Tracy back into his life. It had a sign on the door to his room, but Bill's mind was far away. He didn't notice the sign on the door. He opens the door and slams it behind of him; Jake jumps up out the bed, the girl that's with him screams out. Bill looked over and smiled and kept walking to his side of the room. Jake starts to shout at Bill, that he had someone with him, and that he had a sign on the door. Bill ignores him, and sits on his bed,

"Hey, Bill! Can't you see I had a sign on the door?" shouted Jake.

"Jake just do your business and leave me alone," said Bill

"Bill you full of shit, the girl doesn't feel comfortable with you in here," said Jake

"Well she has a serious problem, she can leave anytime she wants," said Bill

Bill turns his back to them and just lay there thinking about Tracy and how he would get her man out of the way. The girl gets so mad and then pushes Jake off her, and then she takes her clothes to leave the room. Jake was on the floor, very upset at Bill, and he looks over at Bill and screams out loud, and he puts his clothes on. When Jake was leaving the room, he slams the door so hard, and it vibrates through the hallway. Bill was there thinking of all kinds of ways to kill the person from the library. Then it came to him, the man's face had looked familiar to him, but couldn't put his finger on it. It was time for Bill to go to his study group. When he had arrived, everyone in the group was happy to see him. There was a female who liked him, and she was very happy to see him. During the time, she couldn't take her eyes off him; Bill wasn't paying attention to her. Just before the group session was over, she came over and began to talk with Bill. Bill wasn't paying attention; he just wanted to go back to the room and deal with his situation. He quickly brushed her off and left the room. Bill took the usual way back to his room. He was walking past the gym, and saw someone in the pool area of the gym swimming, he stopped and went to look to see who it was. When he looked, it was the same person from the library, and that's why the guy's face was familiar to him. For the next couple of nights, Bill was watching the man at the pool; he notices that the guy would be there by himself. The next night at the study group, Bill was thinking about how he could sneak out without anyone noticing. However, the female who likes him, couldn't take her eyes off him, he knows he had to be quick with it. Bill raises his hand and asks if he could go to the bathroom. When he was going through the door, she stands up and walks through the door with him. Bill was upset, and he walks to the bathroom. Bill looks around the bathroom to see if he could get out without the lady seeing him. There was a little window over the last stall. He had to squeeze through the window to get out; he quickly ran over by the gym. When Bill looks inside, just as before, the guy was swimming alone, Bill looks around to make sure nobody was around. He got inside and waited by the locker room for the boy to come out. One hour passed, and there was no sign of him. Bill walks to the pool area, and the guy was still doing laps in the pool. He was looking around to find something to knock him out.

Bill saw the long broom on the side that's used to clean the pool with, and the man was swimming with his head down. He takes the broom and walks slowly to the edge of the pool, as he swam back to where Bill was standing. As he got near, Bill took the pool broom and slammed it behind his head and then pushed him to the bottom of the pool. He was fighting to get away, but he couldn't. Bill had all his weight on the broom, keeping him pinned to the bottom of the pool. Bill finally felt no struggling from him, and the bubbles stopped. When he lifts up the broom, the guy's body floats to the top. Bill tapped him with the broom. He wanted to make sure the guy was dead, and then Bill wiped his fingerprints off the stick of the broom. When Bill finished, he left to go back to the bathroom; he had to squeeze back through the window. When he came out of the bathroom, the lady was standing there waiting for him. Both of them walked back to the study group. When they walk through the door, everyone had a smile on their faces. The group thought that Bill and she went and did something, Bill was blushing. Bill sits at his chair, and she sits right across from him. Time was near for the study group to be over. She was trying to get his attention when they were finished, Bill got up and went for the door, and she grabs him.

"Hi Bill, I thought that you weren't coming out of the bathroom," said the young woman

"I had a hot one, didn't want to mess myself up in front of everybody," said Bill

"Ha, ha, ha, you are so funny, you know you were coming to this study group for a while and never asked me my name," said the gal.

"Well I am sorry about that, just a lot on my mind, so what's your name," said Bill

"Ok, my is name, Althea," said Althea

"Nice to meet you, Althea, not to cut our conversation short but I have to go, we can pick this up next time," said Bill

Bill rushed through the door. He wanted to be in the room before anyone found the body by the pool. When he reached the room, Bill quickly lies in his bed. As the night went along, he is watching the time. Bill twist and turn through the night. As the light comes through the window, he sits up in the bed. Bill knows that by now, they had found the person's body at the pool. He had a big smile on his face knowing Tracy will come back to him. He quickly got dressed and went through the door. While he was walking to his first class, there was much police on the campus. When he looks over by the gym area, he saw Jake standing over there, so he quickly went over by Jake.

"Hey Jake, what's going on," said Bill

"They found somebody in the pool dead, oh it's you," said Jake

"Wait a minute don't walk off, I am sorry for the other day I just had Tracy on my mind," said Bill

"Bill you really upset me, but you know I can't stay mad with you," said Jake

"So, who did they find in the pool?" said Bill

"I don't know, they say he was swimming and hit his head on the edge of the pool and drown," said Jake

"Poor soul, I hope it isn't someone we know," said Bill

Bill heard someone behind him, and Jake crying when he turned around, it was Tracy. He quickly walks over to Tracy and stands in front of her. When she lifts her head, Tracy saw Bill and puts her arms around him, that was the greatest feeling in the world. Jake watches as it was happening. He knew this is not going to end well; Bill puts his hands around her waist and then walks her back to her room. Bill decided that he wasn't going to any class for today and stays with Tracy. On the way to the room, Tracy held Bill tightly; he was so excited that he had Tracy back in his arms. When Bill got her back in the room, the roommate wasn't there. Tracy asks him to stay with her; Bill smiles and shakes his head. She lay on the bed and reaches out to Bill to come on the bed with her. Bill lies next to her on the bed, Tracy puts her arms around him, he got excited, but Bill knew that now wasn't a good time. He just held her hand. After a while, Tracy had finally fallen asleep; Bill was watching her and passing his fingers through her hair. It was late, and Bill drops asleep too. When Tracy's roommate came into the room it was after midnight. She was surprised to see Bill in the bed with Tracy. She slams the door, Bill jumps up, but Tracy didn't move. When Bill watches the time, it was after midnight already. He got up and put the sheets over Tracy, then went through the door back to his room. As he walks through the door, Bill had a big smile on his face. Bill figures that everything is back on track and by the morning, everything will be okay. Jake was sitting by his desk.

"Well, well what happened to you today," said Jake

"Everything is back on track again with Tracy," said Bill

"Are you sure about that, did she say so?" said Jake

"Not in so many words," said Bill

Jake knew something was wrong about this picture because he remembered what Tracy had told him about a couple of weeks ago. Bill lies in bed, and he couldn't wait until the morning. Jake sits there and watches him. Hoping for his sake that Tracy takes him back because if she doesn't, this just might send him off the edge. The next morning, when Jake opens his eyes, Bill was walking through the door, and Jake tries to stop him. Bill was quick out the door. When he opens the door, Bill was already going down the steps. In front of their building, there was a patch of flowers; Bill picks some and then went to get some breakfast for Tracy. Tracy was happy for the breakfast and the flowers, Bill sat on the ground while Tracy was eating,

"Bill thank you for being there for me," said Tracy

"You know that's not a problem, I will do anything for you," said Bill

"You know the guy that had drown yesterday," asked Tracy

"No, who was that?" said Bill

"It was the guy, I met the other day, he was very nice, and he was a guy in my class, so we decided that we would study together for our upcoming project," said Tracy

"Really, I never saw him before," said Bill

"Come on Bill, you saw him in the library the other day," said Tracy

"You serious, sorry I just overreacted," said Bill

They sat there and talked until it was time for Bill to go to class, he couldn't miss another day of any one of his classes. He told Tracy he would come back to check on her. When

Bill went through the door, he felt like he was on top of the world. As he steps into his class, he went and sat by Althea. She reaches over and tells him hi, Bill's mind was so far that he didn't hear her. All Bill could think of, at that time, was Tracy, Althea reach over and tap him on his shoulder. She began telling him that she had missed him completely yesterday, but Bill looked like he was still in a daze. Althea was still talking, but it was a waste of time, he was watching her in her face, but was picturing it was Tracy.

The teacher shouts out to Bill and Althea to be quiet. At the end of the class, Bill was rushing to go back to Tracy. However, Althea stops him by the door; she asks him if he could walk her to her next class, Bill took and deep breath. He walks her to her next class. Althea had a smile on her face, but Bill didn't know how much Althea liked him. Bill walks her to class and turns away to meet with Tracy, and Althea grabs his hand. She watches him deep in his eyes, and tells him thanks, and leans over and kisses him on the cheek. Bill was a little surprised, but still, it didn't ring a bell; his mind was so into Tracy.

Jake went to the lunchroom to get something to eat when he saw Tracy getting something to eat. He walks over to her,

"Hey girl, what's up?" said Jake

"Just here getting something to eat," said Tracy

"I heard, you lost a friend the other day," said Jake

"Yes, I did, but Bill was there for me, so I am doing a little better now, thanks to him," said Tracy

"Ok if you say so," said Jake

"He understands what a friend truly is," said Tracy

"What you say?" said Jake

Jake explains to Tracy that Bill thinks that they are back together. Tracy opens her eyes in disbelief. She couldn't believe that Bill would think that way. Tracy got up from the table and went back to the room. She sat on the bed waiting for Bill to come over; she's thinking how she would break it down for him. Bill was at his study group; he was looking at his watch the whole time, waiting for the time to finish so that he could be with Tracy. During the class time, Althea was sitting very close to Bill, everyone but Bill knows, that Althea had a crush on him. As soon as they were finished, Bill went rushing through the door; Althea was trying to get his attention. However, he had moved too fast for her, and went through the door, going by Tracy's.

When Bill reaches over by Tracy's dorms, there were many people in the hallways. It looked like one of the girls had a party. There were people all on the floor, passed out, and drugs everywhere. He tries to make it to Tracy's room; he had to step over people to get to her room. Bill reaches the door, and it was locked. He puts his ear on the door. He heard moaning; he pulls his ear quick from the door and watches it in disbelief. Then he puts it again, he heard it again, he starts knocking on the door hard, there was no answer. He knocks on the door again. Still, no answer and the moaning were getting louder. He got so frustrated, and he starts kicking the door. When he got the door open, Bill saw this strange man on top of somebody, and he was stroking away, he got so upset. Bill grabs the man and pulls him off the person and slams him on the ground, when he looks, it wasn't Tracy. The woman starts to scream and curse at him. The man got up off the floor and pushed him out of the room. Bill was laughing to himself as he left and went looking for Tracy. He went room to room looking but didn't find her.

When Bill went outside, he looked over by the Big Tree and saw Tracy talking with this man under the tree. The man who she was talking with had his hand around her waist, and Tracy had a big smile on her face. Bill rushes over there, with fire coming out of his eyes. Tracy and the man didn't see him coming. Bill grabs the man by his hand and pulls him away from Tracy. The man got upset and swung his fist at Bill. Bill duck and came up and held him in a headlock. He starts to squeeze until the man was turning blue in the face. Tracy shouts out to him to stop. Bill looks at Tracy and releases the man. He just drops to the ground, trying to catch his breath.

"Bill! What the hell you are doing," said Tracy

"Who is this punk?" said Bill

"This guy is my friend," said Tracy

"What! What do you mean by a friend, I thought that we were making this work between us?" said Bill

"Well! You thought wrong, I never said that we were back together," said Tracy

"But Tracy I love you," said Bill

"I don't Bill, I don't, you need to leave and don't speak to me again," said Tracy

Tracy helps the man off the ground and walks him to his car. Bill was still there, begging Tracy to give him another chance. It started to rain, and Tracy got into the man's car, Bill was standing there watching her. Tracy tells the man to drive away. Bill was so wet; the rain was mixing in with his tears running down his cheeks. He stood in the rain until he couldn't see the car again. Bill drops to his knees in the mud and couldn't believe what happened. As he was walking to his room in the rain, his flashbacks were getting stronger. He knows that Tracy belongs to him, and he got even angrier.

Chapter 4
Distraction

Bill reaches to his building, he stands by the door, as he was getting wet, Bill reached to open the door, and then suddenly he felt a hand on his shoulder. He smiles because he knew it was Tracy coming back to him. Bill turns around and kisses her, and the person kisses him back. It was raining hard. Bill didn't care about that; he felt that he was on top of the world. When Bill opens his eyes, he quickly jumps back, and it was Althea,

"My God, I am so sorry. I thought you were somebody else," said Bill

"Don't feel bad Bill, come with me, you need to get out of the rain?" said Althea

"Where are we going," said Bill

"To my room," said Althea

Althea had a big smile on her face. As they were walking back to her room, she held Bill tightly around his arm. They finally reached her room; Althea opens the door and tells him to stand on the mat by the door. She went to the bathroom and got a towel for him. Althea rests the towel on the chair next to the door. Althea asks him to remove his wet clothes. Bill wasn't so sure about this, but he was ready to get out of the wet clothes. Bill begins to take his wet clothes off, he was down to his boxers, and Althea was biting her lips. Althea takes the towel and slowly begins to dry him off. Bill's mind was on Tracy the whole time, and he didn't pay attention to Althea. He couldn't get it out of his mind. What Tracy said to him, bothered him, and he couldn't understand why Tracy was acting like that. When Althea was finished drying him, she wraps the towel around him and begins to take off his wet boxers. Bill jumps, and saw Althea on her knees, pulling on his boxers, and then he realizes he had the towel around him. He smiles at Althea and takes off his boxers; Althea went for one of her bathrobes, she puts it on him, Althea tells him to go and lay on her bed. Bill sits on the edge of her bed; he takes a couple of deep breaths and then lays on her bed.

Bill couldn't accept what Tracy had told him tonight. The image of Tracy stepping in the car with the guy repeatedly plays in his head, and the man was laughing at him. Bill could h see himself choking the life out of him. Althea came back into the room with dry clothes for him. Bill sits up on the bed, and he smiles at Althea and goes to the bathroom. Althea tiptoes over to the bathroom, she kneels down, and peeks through the keyhole, he was naked. She couldn't believe the body Bill had, and the package he was carrying, she was taking deep breaths. As he finished dressing, Bill begins to walk toward the door, Althea ran, and jumps into the bed. Bill came out and walked over to the bed; he bent down and kissed Althea on her forehead. He tells her thanks for everything she had done for him tonight and tells her he has to leave. Althea didn't want him to leave, but Bill took his wet clothes and went through the door.

When Bill got back to his room, he stood by the door for a while before he opened it. When He entered the room, Bill walks past Jake without saying anything to him; Jake figured that Tracy had told him what she told him earlier. Also, that he didn't take it well, Jake tells Bill he is going to the soda machine to get a soda and come back. As Jake reaches the machine, he calls Tracy,

"Hey girl, what's up?" said Jake

"Hi Jake, I am just here," said Tracy

"Did you tell Bill," asked Jake

"Yes, I did, after he rushed the guy who I was talking with, I had to pull him off the guy. I got so upset, I tell him that we are not together, and will never be together again" said Tracy

They were there for a while talking, and then Jake warned her to be careful with Bill. His emotions were very rocky, and that something was strange about him, Jake hung up and went back upstairs. When he was going up the stairs, Bill was coming down the stairs; Jake stops him and asks him where he was going. He tells Jake; he was just going for a walk. Bill kept walking; he didn't look at Jake. Jake didn't like that idea, so he ran up to Bill and asked him if he could come along. Bill tells him no; he just wanted to be by himself right now. Jake went back to the room.

Bill walks for hours around the campus, he has a lot going through his mind, and he finds himself back by Tracy's. He was right under the big tree looking into Tracy's room. He saw her getting herself ready for bed. Bill was trying to figure out a way to get back with her. As he was going to turn away, he saw her stand up and open her arms, and then saw the same person from earlier, hug her and start to kiss her. Bill's heart was racing fast; he couldn't breathe; Bill drops to one knee to catch himself.

He got up and began punching the tree; he was hitting the tree so hard that a piece of the bark came off the tree. His hand was bloody. One of the securities was walking by at that moment, he saw Bill under the tree, the security calls out to him, but Bill runs across the street to one of the frat houses. Bill hides from the security, when the security walks past the frat house and didn't see him, the security left the area. Bill decided to stay there until the person leaves from Tracy's. About two hours pass, the person finally came out. He follows the person to another frat house a couple of houses down the block; he stands across the street looking into the frat house. For the next couple of days, Bill follows the person everywhere, even when the person meets up with Tracy. Bill would watch them having fun and get upset to the point that he couldn't breathe. One day, Tracy and the person were sitting under the tree, and Bill was across the street, hiding in the bushes watching them. When they got up and were walking away, Bill steps out of the bushes and begins to follow them. At that same time, Althea was walking up the road towards him, Bill didn't see her, but she saw him. Althea runs, and hugs him from behind, Bill jumps and turns around.

"Hi Bill, long time no see' said Althea

"Just been busy, working on stuff," said Bill

"I haven't seen you from the night you been by me, I hope I didn't make you feel funny in any way," said Althea

"No, Althea, just I had a lot on my mind that night, nothing to do with you. I would have liked to talk some more with you, but I had to go" said Bill

Bill kisses her on her cheek, and then he went looking for Tracy and the person. Althea was feeling great at that time. Bill looks everywhere for them but couldn't find them anywhere. Jake saw Bill looking like he lost something, so he walks over to Bill and asks him if he was ok. Bill answered him coldly and kept on walking. Jake knew something was wrong with him; he calls Tracy to make sure she was okay. Bill couldn't find them, and that upset him even more, so he gave up for the night and went back to his room. When Bill enters his building, a person was handing out flyers for a party at one of the frat houses. Bill grabbed the flyer out of his hand and went to his room; Jake was at his desk studying. Bill walked in, slammed the door, and went straight to his bed. Jake tries to talk to him, but he wasn't saying anything, Bill opens the flyer, begins to read it. He had one big smile on his face. The party was at the same person's frat house.

The night of the party, Jake was leaving the room, and Bill was still in his bed. Before Jake was leaving, he asks Bill if he was coming, Bill shakes his head no, so Jake left and went to the party. Bill got up and looks through the window to make sure Jake had left. He put some clothes on, and then went through the door. Then, Bill stood across the street, hoping that someone comes outside for something. At that moment, he sees the person and two others come outside. Bill moves closer to them; he was right behind a car down from them. He overheard the two people telling the person how many cases of beer they need him to pick up. Bill knows this was his chance. The person jumped into his car and drove off.

Bill picks up a brick to break the car glass he was hiding behind. As he was going to break the glass, he notices the keys were in the ignition. When he lifts the handle for the door, it unlocked, and Bill quickly jumps into the car and follows the person to the liquor store. The person pulls up in front of the store and runs inside, and Bill reverses right behind him. About ten minutes later, the guy came out with a couple of cases; he opens his trunk and starts to pack the beers. He went back inside for the last of the cases; the person didn't notice the car behind him was on. As he bends over to put the last case in the trunk, Bill puts the car in reverse, and mash on the gas pedal.

By the time the person realizes what was happening, the car slams into him, crushing him between the two cars. Then Bill drives forward, and the guy drops to the ground; he was screaming in pain. His hips were crushed, and his legs were broken. Bill opens the door and watches the guy in his face, when the guy sees who it was, his eyes open wide. Bill smiles, gets back into the care and reverses on the guy again, crushing his head, his brains, and blood splattering all over the road. The man in the store came running out. Bill puts the car in drive and mashes the gas, speeding away from the liquor store. The store owner couldn't see who was driving the car.

As Bill was driving away, he had a big smile on his face, but he didn't realize the guy's body was stuck up under the car. Just as he reached close to the college, he pulls off the road and parks the car in the bushes. Bill took a cloth and wiped the whole inside of the car; he didn't want to leave any fingerprints. He walks around the car to get out of the bushes, and he trips over something in the bushes. When Bill looks down to see what it was, he laughs aloud; it was the person's body. It was in pieces, with all of his guts hanging out.

Bill tries to sneak back to the room, but Jake saw him. It was strange to him, noticing what time it was. He was outside talking with some of his friends when two guys came outside, looking very upset. They were waiting for the beers, but the guy didn't come back as yet, so they send another guy to get the beers. Jake tries to listen to what they were saying but couldn't hear clearly. The guys went back inside, while the next guy went for the beers. A little while after, Tracy came outside looking very worried; Jake walks over to her.

"Hey Tracy, you look worried," said Jake

"Yes, I am, my friend hasn't come back as yet," said Tracy

"Who is that?" asked Jake

"The one they send for the beers earlier, "said Tracy

Jake pauses and thinks back to Bill, and then he remembers seeing Bill sneaking into the building earlier. Tracy saw the expression on Jake's face and asks him if he knows something about her friend. Jake tells her no and reassures her he was ok and tells her that he should be back soon. Tracy went back inside. Jake sits on the steps to wait for the person to come back; he was outside alone. Then he sees a car coming from a distance; he begins to feel relieved when the car pulls up. The other person who was sent for the beers had returned; it only took him about twenty minutes to come back. Now he started getting worried. When the guy went inside with the beers, everyone starts cheering. About two minutes after, Tracy came back outside; Jake sees the look on her face and knows she was worried now. Jake puts his arms around her, she was shaking, and both of them sit on the steps waiting for her friend.

Bill was across the street between one of the frat houses, watching Jake and Tracy. They were close to each other, Tracy's head was on Jake's shoulder, and Jake's arms were around her. Bill felt his head pulsating, and his eyes were blood red, and then from a distance, Tracy and Jake see a flashing light coming towards them. Bill slipped back between the frat houses and went back to his room. Bill takes off his clothes and lies in bed. About twenty minutes, Bill heard the music stop. About three minutes after, he heard Tracy screaming out. Bill laughs to himself; the police had found the car. The police drive onto the campus to ask anybody if they had recognized the car. When Tracy saw the picture of the car, she fainted. In the picture, you could see the blood on the trunk of the car. Everyone was coming outside; Jake held Tracy before she fell to the ground.

From a distance, Tracy sees her friend walking up the street, she pushes Jake off and runs to her friend. She squeezes him tightly. Everyone started mumbling to themselves wondering who was really in the car. Even the police were confused. Tracy's friend was puzzled by everyone's sad and depressed attitude. He was upset that he had to walk back to the college. Tracy starts to explain it to him. Her friend drops to his knees and starts to cry. The police came over and helped him up, and then pulled him to the side to get some answers.

"Young man, what's your name?" asks the police officer.

"My name is Jeffry, sir."

"Now explain to us what happened," said the police officer Jeffry begins to explain, on his way to buy the beers; he had to make a quick stop by his cousin's house to use the bathroom. Therefore, he asks his cousin to make the beer run for him and pick him back up. However, a couple of hours had passed, so he decided to walk back to the campus. The police explain to him how they find his cousin's body under the car. They also explain that they run the plates and find out that the car belongs to a student here. Jeffry asks who it was, but they couldn't give him that information. The police send him back to Tracy. Jeffrey couldn't catch himself; he was still in disbelief; Jeffrey explains to her it was his cousin. Then it flashes in her head, that someone was trying to kill him; she went over by the police and told them what she was thinking. They just brushed her off, the police had located the owner of the car, and they went with him.

At that time, the sun was coming up. Jake went back to the room to take a bath. He got ready and went through the door to his classes. As he was going through the door, he looks at Bill lying on the bed; he had a strong feeling that Bill knew something. When Bill heard the door close, he turns over and looks through the window at Jake walking to class. Bill got up and went into the shower; he was singing and feeling good; he left the room to go to his classes. Everyone he passes was looking sad. He was laughing to himself; when Bill was passing the frat house, there was a black ribbon on the door, Bill even laughs some more. As Bill was stepping in the building to go to his first class, he sees Tracy coming through the door. He went to comfort her. When he saw her friend came out from behind her and put his arms around, Bill stops and steps back with eyes wide open. Tracy saw him and went to say hi to him. Bill turns around and walks away. Tracy was confused. Jeffery held her by hand.

Bill went back to the room, he couldn't understand, and it didn't make any sense to him. He knew that he killed him last night, but how was it possible that he was alive. For hours and hours, Bill just sits there, trying to understand it. Jake walks back into the room to get one of his books. He saw Bill was looking puzzled,

"Hey Bill, you ok?" asked Jake

"Something isn't adding up," said Bill

"I know what you mean, the same thing happened to us last night, we thought Jeffery was dead," said Jake

"Who is Jeffery?" said Bill

"Tracy's friend, we thought he was the one that got killed last night, but it was his cousin," said Jake

The expression on Bill's face changes, Jake saw the expression on his face; it was as if he saw the devil in him. Jake didn't like that look, so for the next couple of days, he followed Bill around the campus, and to his study group.

Chapter 5
The New Love

When Bill went to his study group. Jake stood outside, looking in. As he watched, one thing he noticed, that this girl Althea was into Bill, she couldn't take her eyes off of him. They had just finished, and everyone was going through the door; Jake went behind the wall and waited until all of them were gone. He follows Althea until she had reached her building as she was going inside. Jake pulls her aside,

"Excuse me, can I have a word with you," said, Jake

"Can I help you?" said Althea

"Do you know Bill?" said Jake

For hours they were talking, Jake couldn't believe how much she knows about Bill. Jake invited Althea over to the room, and he wanted to surprise Bill. When Jake reaches back to the room, Bill was in his bed. Jake took off his clothes and laid in the bed, but Bill was still up. He waited until Jake drops to sleep; Bill had a knife in his hand, and then he walked over to Jake's bed. Bill stands over him, watching him while squeezing the knife in his hand. He wanted to stab Jake so bad, but he couldn't right now. He didn't have an alibi. Therefore, he went back into his bed and watched Jake all through the night.

That morning Jake was leaving the room, and he asks Bill if he was going to his classes today. Bill did not respond to him, so Jake left the room, Bill was in another world, thinking about how to kill him. He thought that Tracy would get closer to Jeffery because of his cousin. Bill couldn't stomach the thought that someone else would have Tracy; he begins to stab the bed up. Jake walks back into the room because he had forgotten something, and saw that look on Bill's face, as if the devil was smiling, Jake rushes out of the room. He knew something was up with Bill. Jake left and went to look for Tracy. Bill gets up and looks to put on clothes, but he realizes all his clothes were dirty. Therefore, he packed up his clothes and went to the little laundry room the campus had.

As Bill puts his clothes in the machine to wash, Jeffery just walks into the laundry. Bill's pulse was racing; he wanted to bash his head in right there, so he starts looking around for something. He notices a piece of the pipe behind the dryer. Jeffery puts his clothes in the machine close to Bill's. Jeffery begins to talk to Bill, Bill thought Jeffery was crazy, but his back was turned to Jeffery. Jeffery walks closer to Bill, and puts his hand on his shoulders; right away Bill knocks his hand off his shoulder

"Hey what's your problem?" said Jeffery

"You don't remember me, but I remember you, I was the one that kicks your ass under the tree the other night," said Bill

"You little punk, that's right, you sucker-punched me, and your ex-girl had to save you. I should kick your ass now," said Jeffery

Jeffery steps closer to Bill, and Bill steps back to reach for the pipe behind the dryer. Jeffery rushes Bill, as he got closer, Bill takes the pipe and swings the pipe, and hits Jeffery down to the ground. Bill stood over him and looked to swing the pipe again. At that same time, Jake walks into the laundry. Jake saw Jeffery on the ground, he ran and jumped between both of them. Bill throws the pipe on the ground. Then Bill walks away, he was so upset with Jake for stopping him from beating Jeffery. Bill said to himself that he should have killed Jake last night. He went straight back to the room and waited for Jake to come back. This time he was going to kill him, Bill pulls the knife from between his bed; suddenly he heard the doorknob turning. When the door opens, Bill gets up and rushes the door, grabs him from behind the door. Bill slams him against the wall and was looking to drive the knife in his stomach.

"Bill what are you doing?" said Althea

"OH shit! Althea! What are you doing here?" said Bill

"Your friend invited me over," said Althea

"Jake!" said Bill

Bill sits on his bed, and then Althea sits next to him; she asks what was going on with him and his friend. Bill tells her they were playing a game and she walked in on it, Althea believed him. Bill was curious as to how Althea knows Jake. Althea explains how they met after their study group yesterday. She tells him everything, and Bill wasn't pleased about that. At that same time, Jake walked into the room and saw both of them on the bed. Bill watches Jake funny, and Jake knew he was mad about earlier. Bill tells Jake that he and Althea were going. They walk out of the room, Jake was a little scared of Bill, because many things didn't add up with him.

After Jake's last class of the day, he went over by Tracy; she was very upset after what Jeffery had told her. Tracy didn't want to talk with Bill again. Tracy and Jake went under the big tree.

"You believe the shit with Bill, Jeffery told me everything," said Tracy

"If I didn't walk in at the time, I think Bill would have killed him," said Jake

"I think Bill is not that crazy, Jake," said Tracy

"If you had been there, you'd be saying something different now, I just want you to be careful Tracy," said Jake

Bill knew that Jake didn't trust him, and he knew by now he would tell Tracy about the incident at the laundry with Jeffery. He had to come from another angle with Jeffery, and Jake, so Bill decided to hang out with Althea more, to the point everyone thought they were together. Tracy was relieved that Bill was seeing someone. Therefore, he could get over his obsession with her, Jake was a little happy, but still didn't trust him.

The night after their study group, Althea was very happy, because the last couple of days, she had Bill to herself. Althea invited Bill over to her room, and she was very excited. Althea couldn't wait to get Bill all to herself when they reach her room. Bill asks her to use the bathroom, Althea shows him the bathroom and sits on the bed. She was all excited about Bill being in her room; in the bathroom, Bill was watching himself in the mirror. As he took a couple of deep breaths, and then he came out. Bill sits by her computer desk; Althea walks over by him. She stands in front of him. Althea puts her hands on his head, and then Bill rests his head on her breasts. He slowly puts his arms around her waist; Bill raises his head to kiss her. Althea bends down to him, as her lips get close, she pushes him away and tells him she is going to the bathroom. Althea rushes into the bathroom, Bill sits in the chair, wondering if he should do this, because he couldn't get Tracy out of his head, and then the door opens. Althea was in a towel. His eyes open wide, she walks slowly over to Bill, and she stands right in front of him. Althea drops her towel, Bill's mouth opens wide, he couldn't believe the body she had. She puts her hand under his chin and stands him up. Althea slowly undresses Bill, when she takes off his pants, Bill was very excited. Althea walks him over by the bed and lies him down on it; Bill adjusts himself up more in the bed. Althea climbs onto the bed and stands over him, and then she sits on him.

"Bill, I wanted you, from the first time I had seen you, every night I dream about you being in my bed. I don't want you to say a word, just let me pleasure you for the night" said Althea

Bill didn't say anything, he closed his eyes and imagined it was Tracy's, every kiss, every touch. When Althea's body rubbed against his, it was Tracy's body. In the middle of it, Bill calls out Tracy's name. Althea pauses and watches him, and then she continues, she was happy she had Bill where she wanted him. For each time he called Tracy's name, Althea went with the flow. Althea answers him, the more she answers him, the more passionate Bill became. After they were finished, Althea laid on Bill's arms with a smile on her face. After a while, Althea drops asleep. Bill was up looking at the ceiling, thinking about Tracy. It was getting close to morning; he slips himself from under Althea. He quickly puts on his clothes and then left the room. Bill was walking down the hallway as he was passing by Tracy's door; Bill stops and stands by the door. Therefore a while, Bill was going to knock on the door, but he changed his mind, Bill went out through the back, and stands under the big tree. He stood there watching into her room, with tears in his eyes, as the sun was coming up, Bill walked away from the tree and went to his room. When he enters the room, Jake had a female sleeping in the bed with him; again, he couldn't do anything to Jake. Bill went into his bed, lies there watching Jake, when Jake opened his eyes and saw Bill watching him, Jake sits up in the bed and looks at Bill; Jake asked him if everything was ok, Bill got up, and walked out the room, Jake knew from this point he had to watch his back with Bill.

As the week's pass, Bill was trying to figure out a way to kill Jeffery, every time he tried, Althea would pop up everywhere. She always wanted to be up under him; a couple of times, Tracy and Jeffery cross paths with Bill and Althea. Tracy would have a smile on her face because she was happy that Bill moved on. Even after the study group, Althea would come over by Bill's room, Whenever Jake sees Althea walk into the room, he would leave. Bill was getting upset, but he had to hold his cool so that no one would suspect anything with him.

Jeffery still didn't like Bill, and he wanted to get back at him from that night under the tree, and by the laundry. Jeffery was talking with some of his friends, and they were planning to jump him and beat the crap out of him. For days, Jeffery had someone follow Bill around and monitor his girlfriend. Then, word got back to Jeffery that Bill and his girlfriend were going to the movies Saturday night. Jeffery and his friends planned for Bill; Jeffery invited Tracy to go to the movies with him. When Saturday night finally came, Jeffery had his friends go to the same movie that Bill and Althea went to. Also, he and Tracy went to a different movie. In the middle of the movie, Bill got up to go to the bathroom. Jeffery's friends got up and went behind him; Bill went into one of the stalls to urinate. Jeffery's friends softly walk into the bathroom and lock the door. Bill didn't hear them come in. As Bill turns around to go and wash his hands, one of them kicks him in his chest, slamming him against the wall. Then the next one grabs him, pulls him out of the stall, and pushes him on the ground, the rest of them stand around him. They began stomping on him; all Bill could do was cover his head. When they were finished, all of them took out their penises and began peeing on him. One bends down and whispers in his ear,

"You better stay away from Jeffery and Tracy or else," said the guy

Althea was getting worried that Bill had not returned from the bathroom. She got up to look for him, and she went straight to the bathroom area. When she walks around the corner, she saw Bill crawling out of the bathroom; He had blood all over his face and smelled like urine. Althea screams out, the employees, and the manager came running. The manager sends one of his employees to call the police, and the police and the ambulance came within minutes. Tracy starts to hear the sirens loud, so did everyone else in the theater; everyone begins to come outside to see what had happened. Jeffery and Tracy came out; there were a lot of people in the hallway. Tracy couldn't see what was going on. When Jeffery and Tracy were walking away, Tracy saw Althea in the corner crying. She finds it strange; she begins to think that something had happened to Bill. The employees for the theater start to chase everyone back inside; the ambulance leaves quickly with Bill.

When the ambulance reaches the hospital, Althea calls Jake and lets him know what had happened to Bill. Jake quickly puts on his clothes and rushes over by the hospital. Upon his arrival, Jake sees Althea in the lobby.

"Hey girl, you ok, and what the hell is going on," said Jake

"I don't know Jake, Bill went to the bathroom, but he was taking so long, I `went to look for him. Then I see him crawling out of the bathroom". Said, Althea

 Jake and Althea were there for a while. When the police came, Jake and Althea were still in the lobby. The police passed them straight and went and asked the nurse which room Bill was in. The doctor was just leaving the room. There were two nurses left in the room, and the officer asks them to leave the room. When they left the room, the officer begins to question Bill; Bill was hesitating to say anything to the officer. He wanted to get back at the guys who did this to him. He told the officers that he couldn't see the faces and that it was dark. The officers see it as a dead-end; they left the room and let the nurses back in. Jake and Althea were standing by the door to go in to see Bill; the nurse tells them to wait for a couple of minutes then they could enter. When Althea sees Bill with his face bandaged up, she starts crying. Jake was feeling sorry for Bill. Jake walks over to Bill and asks him if he knew who had done this to him. Bill wasn't saying much, and he just wanted to get out of the hospital. Althea stays at his side, while Jake walks out of the room to give Tracy a call. Tracy was over by Jeffery's relaxing from the movie, Jeffery heard her phone ring in her bag; Tracy was asleep on his chest. He reaches over and went into her bag; he sees it was Jake calling. Jeffery rejects the call and turns off the phone. Jake was getting upset. He tries and tries again, this time it went straight to voice mail. After he couldn't get through, Jake went back into the room with Althea and Bill. Althea was sitting by Bill's bedside, with her head on his chest. Jake pulls the chair close to the door and sits down. Bill was looking straight up to the ceiling; Jake saw the anger in Bill's face, knowing to himself that Bill wasn't going to leave it alone. Just like that, Jake dozed off in the chair, Althea was asleep on his chest, Bill was too angry to sleep, and he plays how the guys beat him in the bathroom repeatedly in his head, he marks each one of their faces. About ten in the morning, the doctor walks into the room, he explains to Jake and Althea that Bill would be able to leave in a couple of hours. That was the only time Bill had a smile on his face; Jake didn't like that smile on his face. Althea was very excited; she would be able to cuddle with Bill. Jake tries again to call Tracy. Still, he had no luck. After a couple of hours had passed, The nurse came back in with his discharge papers; Bill was ordered to take a couple more days from his classes to rest. Also, to stay off his feet as much as possible. Bill was in front, leading them through the door. He wanted to find the guys who jumped him. While Jake was driving back to the college, Bill was staring out the window, Althea was leaning on his chest, and Jake was watching him from the rearview mirror. He knew Bill was plotting something, and he was upset with Tracy. The number of messages he left on her phone, and Tracy did not call him back. It was already afternoon, and Jake couldn't understand it. They finally pulled up by Jake and Bill's building; Althea held onto Bill when they were walking up the stairs. When they reached the room, Bill tells them that he wanted to be alone, but Althea insisted that she stay. Jake left them in the room and went to look for Tracy. When he reached over by her room, he was knocking on the door hard. Jake was really upset with Tracy for not answering her phone, as the door opens, it was her roommate.

"Where the hell is Tracy," said Jake

"The first thing you need to do stops shouting, the second thing, morning to you too. The third and last thing is" said the roommate

She slams the door, and shouts out that Tracy wasn't there, Jake was pissed the hell off. Only one place Jake could think of, that Tracy would be right now, by Jeffery's. Jake storms over by Jeffery's frat house. When he was walking down the sidewalk, Tracy was coming out of the house. He runs up beside her and pulls her aside. When he looks up by the house, Jeffery was standing on the porch; he whispers to Tracy that they needed to talk. Tracy tells Jeffery she would talk with him later and goes with Jake up the road; Jeffery had a grin on his face. He knew what Jake was going to tell Tracy, he laughed to himself and went inside. Jeffery calls all his frat members from upstairs to come down to the living room. When everyone was there, he begins to explain that Jake was telling Tracy about what had happened to Bill. Everybody starts to laugh, and

Jeffery was smiling, he warns everyone to be careful out there. His frat members ask if they could do something to Jake, Jeffery says no, because he was Tracy's best friend.

Chapter 6
One-By- One

Jake was pulling on Tracy, trying to reach her room as fast as possible. When they reach her room, the roommate was leaving at the same time; she watches Jake from head to toe and blows off, then walks off. Jake sticks up his middle finger. Tracy watches him funny and asks him what had happened between them. Jake tells her nothing and pushes her into the room. Tracy was curious about what Jake had to tell her. Jake sits her down on her bed and begins to explain to her what had happened to Bill. Tracy got up and starts to argue with Jake, why he didn't call her, Jake eyes open wide,

"What the hell, I was calling your phone from the time I got to the hospital," said Jake

"Yeah right, my phone didn't ring, and if it did, I would have heard it," said Tracy

"Well you need to check your phone?" said Jake

Tracy took the phone out of her bag to show Jake that she didn't have any missed calls from him. Her phone was off, she was puzzled, couldn't remember turning off her phone, and it was very strange to her. When she turns on her phone, she notices that Jake called her phone four times. However, didn't remember hearing the phone was ringing, Tracy was a puzzled again. She tells Jake she wanted to go over to see Bill; Jake pauses, Tracy asks him what happened. He explains that Althea was over there with him. Tracy tells him that she didn't care; they left her room and went over by Bill's. As they reach by Bill's, Jake opens the door, and Althea smiles, when Tracy walks through the door, as Althea saw Tracy, she stands up.

"What the hell is she doing here," said Althea

"She, my name is Tracy," said Tracy

"Calm down Althea, we all grew up together, she has the right to be here. She just wanted to see how he was doing," said Jake

Bill sits up in the bed, and holds Althea by her hand, and tells her it's ok, but Althea didn't want to move from in front of Bill. He squeezes her hand and asks her to give Tracy a chance; Jake and Althea went into the hallway.

"How you are doing," said Tracy (with tears in her eyes)

"Could be better, and you?" said Bill

"I am so sorry I wasn't there with you last night," said
Tracy

"It's ok, Tracy you were with your man, don't worry about
me, Althea is here for me," said Bill

Tracy was feeling bad; she leans over to kiss him on his
forehead, but Bill pulls away. Tracy gets up and walks to
the door; she looks back at Bill with tears in her eyes. As
she walks out of the door, Althea sees that she had tears
running down her cheeks, she smiles. Tracy walks past her
and Jake. Jake tries to stop her, but she pulls away from
him. Tracy went running to her building; she was feeling
bad that she wasn't there for Bill. There was a little
jealousy for Althea; she lies in her bed, crying for a couple
of minutes. Her phone was ringing, it was Jake calling to
check on her, and she picks up the phone and tells him that
she would talk with him tomorrow, hearing her voice, Jake
knew she was crying.

For the next couple of days, it was Bill and Althea
everywhere. Althea's feelings were getting stronger. How
Bill feels for Althea, he sees her as a good friend; his heart
still belongs to Tracy. He had felt bad about what he had to
tell Tracy the time she came to see him. He was mad with
her at that time. As time passed, he had realized what he

did to her. By the second week, he was finally feeling much better. Bill left the room for the first time to head to his classes. When he was walking by the library, Jeffery and his friends were standing outside handing out flyers. They were having a party at the frat house this coming weekend, but when they see Bill, all of them begin to laugh at him. Bill just keeps his head straight and continues walking. When he reaches to his first class, there was one of the frat members sitting by him with the flyer in his hand.

Bill pulls the flyer out of the frat member's hand when he sees that the party is this weekend. He recognizes the person from the bathroom at the movie; his mind begins working and plotting. The next day, he and Althea were walking past the frat house, and Jeffery and all the frat members were sitting on the porch. All of them were laughing aloud; Althea would wonder why they would laugh like that. Bill responded by telling her, they were jerks and keeps walking. The day of the party, Bill was walking past the house, Tracy and Jeffery were on the porch, Tracy puts her head down, as the guys were laughing, Althea was watching Tracy hard. One of the guys jump off the porch and approaches Althea, and he stands in front of her.

"Hey sweetness, why you are walking with this loser," said the guy

"YOU need to step away from her now," said Bill

The guy laughs in Bill's face and puts his hands on Althea's shoulder; Althea swings her leg so hard kicking him so hard between his legs, he drops to his knees and starts screaming like a girl. All of his friends on the porch were laughing at him; Bill smiles, holds Althea's hand, and steps over the guy on the ground.

As the time gets closer to the party at Jefferys, Jake begins to get ready for the party; Bill was on the bed relaxing with Althea at his side. When Jake finishes getting dressed, he asks Bill if he was coming, Bill watches him funny and shakes his head. Jake knew he and Jeffery had bad blood between them but thought he would have come with Althea. Jake left the room when he reaches outside of the building, the music was playing loud, and there were a lot of people outside. Bill's mind was running with all kinds of ideas; he wanted to go over there and light the house on fire. However, he didn't want other people to get hurt because of the frat members, he tells Althea to go ahead, and go back to her room because he was tired. Althea didn't want to go, she wanted to stay with him, but Bill insisted that she go. After she left, Bill went by the window and watched her until she was out of sight. He quickly dressed in all back and waited for another two hours, and he climbs out of the window. Bill went to the end of the frat house and sat to wait for someone to come outside. About forty minutes passed until one of the people came out the back, the person was very drunk. The person went to the side of the house to pee; as he starts peeing, Bill steps into the light. The person jumps back and pees all over himself. He gets so mad; He went up in Bill's face.

Moreover, he was shouting at him; Bill punches him in his stomach, the person drops to his knees. Bill stands behind him and puts his arms around his neck and begins to squeeze until the person passes out. Bill lifts him and carries him over by the library; he carries him to the top of the library roof. He had a syringe full of heroin; he takes the guy's arm and squeezes until he sees a vein; he takes the syringe full of heroin, then squeezes the whole syringe into his arm. Bill waited for a couple of minutes until the heroin started to take effect on him. The person began shaking on the ground; Bill picks the person up and throws him off the roof. When his body hits the ground, it exploded like a rotten tomato, his head splits open, and there was blood everywhere. Bill watches over the edge, and he laughs to himself, then Bill went straight back to his room.

The campus security was patrolling; as he was getting close to the library, he sees something at the front. As he gets closer, it looked like a dummy on the ground. He begins to laugh to himself. Thinking that the students were playing games, he stops the car and slowly walks toward the dummy. There was blood around it; he shakes his head, thinking the students went to the extreme with it. When the security stood over the dummy and looked hard at it, it started to look more real to him. The security bent down and touched the blood around it; it felt and smelled like real blood. Then he pokes his finger in the brain that was coming out of the dummy's head, and then he realizes it was a body. He immediately runs back into the car and calls for back up; the security puts his head out the car then begins to throw up. By the time he catches himself, the rest of the security had arrived. They called the police right away; it takes them about ten minutes to respond to the call. When the police reach the campus, they heard the loud music coming from Jeffery's party. Two officers went over by the party and knocked on the door. When the person opened the door and saw it was the police, they run away from the door, running through the party shouting, Police! Everyone begins to scramble for the back door. Nevertheless, there were two more officers at the back door; nobody could get out. Then the officers gather everyone in the living room, Jeffery was very upset that they stopped the party. Everyone wanted to know what was going on, one by one, the officers call each of them into the kitchen to question them. After they question each student, they let them out the back. After the fourth student was questioned, texts started to alert the rest of them inside the house. Everyone was shocked that someone had gotten killed. However, they didn't know who it was that got killed. After the officers finish questioning everyone, they send everyone on their way. Jake rushes back to the room, when he opens the door, Bill was in his bed sleeping; Jake shake Bill until he was up,

"What the hell, Jake!" said Bill

"Someone got killed on campus," said Jake

"So, what that has to do with me, don't you see I am sleeping," said Bill

"Bill, you don't have to be so cold," said Jake

Bill turned back over in his bed and had a smile on his face; Jake didn't like the feeling he was getting from Bill. Jake lies in his bed and watches Bill for a while when Bill turns in his direction; Jake closes his eyes. After the officers left the house, Jeffery and the rest of the members of the house sit down. They were trying to figure out who was the one that got killed. Tracy noticed that one of his friends was missing; she begins to ask Jeffery for one of his friends. Jeffery sends the rest of the members to look for him around the house and outside. They couldn't find him, they went back to Jeffery's and let him know, Tracy saw the worried look on his face. He tells everyone and Tracy to wait there for him. Jeffery left the house and went over by the officers. Jeffery asks the officers if he could see the body; at first, the officers were giving him a hard time to see the body. Jeffery explains that one of his friends was missing, and he wanted to make sure he was ok. When they lift the sheet, you couldn't recognize the face on the body, but when Jeffery saw the shoes, he dropped to his knees, he couldn't breathe. The officer helps him off the ground; Jeffery tells the officer that is his friend, the officers went back over to Jeffery's frat house. When Jeffery walks through the door, he had tears in his eyes; once everyone sees that, they knew it was their friend. The officers questioned them one by one again, trying to find out who saw him last. Jeffery was all broken up about it; he rested his head on Tracy's lap and was crying. Tracy was feeling sad for him. She wanted to call Jake right away and tell him. When the officers were done with everyone, she takes Jeffery upstairs and puts him in bed. When he finally fell asleep, Tracy left the house.

 As she was walking back to her building, Tracy calls Jake and tells him that it was one of Jeffery's friends that were killed. Jake looks over at Bill; he begins to believe Bill had something to do with it. Bill's eyes were open, listening to Jake on the phone; he knew it was Tracy on the phone with him. Jake got up and went out of his room; he didn't want to wake Bill up as he closes the door. Tracy and Jake were on the phone for a long time, until Bill gets up and stands by the door; he was listening to them. He overheard Jake saying that Jeffery was crying, Bill burst out laughing, then he didn't hear Jake anymore. The doorknob starts to turn. Bill jumps in his bed and picks up his phone, play like he was talking with Althea. Jake opened the door and saw him on the phone and went back outside; Bill was laughing aloud.

 Two days had passed, the campus was quiet to the point nobody did not say anything about the killing. At the frat house, didn't have much movement, everyone was just sitting around. Then there was a knock at the door; it was someone from the Dean's office when Jeffery reaches the

Dean's office. He saw the officer sitting there; the Dean
tells him to sit down.

"Jeffery, I need you to listen to what the officer has to say,"
said the Dean

"What's wrong now?" said Jeffery

"You need to relax now, Jeffery," said the officer

The officers begin to explain to him that the reports came
back, that his friend's blood was full of heroin. Jeffery
stands up and shouts that it was a lie, the Dean tries to get
Jeffery under control. The officer gets up and pushes
Jeffery back in the chair; he shows him the reports,
showing him what it found was. Jeffery explains that his
friend doesn't do drugs; the officer tells him that he didn't
know his friend as good as he thought. Jeffery storms out of
the office slams the door, he went straight back to the frat
house. Jeffery explains what the police tell him, everyone
was shocked, because he was the only one in the house who
didn't do any drugs.

As the days pass, Jeffery and Tracy, and the rest of the
members would be on the porch. There were other days
when Bill would pass in front of the house; he would have
a big smile on his face. Some of the members of the house
would get upset and throw words at him. One day while
Tracy was there, one of Jeffery's friends came off the porch

and rushed in front of Bill. Bill walks around the friend, and everyone on the porch laughed, even Jeffery. Jeffery calls the friend back on the porch, Tracy got suspicious of that; they begin to call him names and to spit at him. Tracy looks at Jeffery, gets his attention to let them stop, but Jeffery was laughing aloud. She gets mad and storms into the house, Jeffery runs behind her.

"Jeffery, what is going on with your friends and Bill," said Tracy

"What are you talking about baby?" said Jeffery

"Each time Bill walks by the house, your friends shout at him, and then today they look to beat him up," said Tracy

"You know how the guys get, that's just the guys baby," said Jeffery

"Do you know, who jumped Bill at the movie?" said Tracy

Jeffery pauses for a second and tells her he didn't know; Tracy looks him straight in his face. She didn't believe him. Tracy kisses him on his forehead and goes to class. On her way to her class, Tracy calls Jake and asks him to meet her by the library after her class. Jake was in the room when Tracy had called; when he said ok to Tracy, Bill looks around at him. Jake grabs his stuff and left the room; Bill had a feeling that it was Tracy on the phone. He wanted to kill Jake, but he knew he had to be careful with him, and he had to deal with Jeffery and his friends. He was trying to think of a way, how to kill Jeffery, and then it hit him; Althea was taking forensic sciences. Bill gets out of bed and gets dressed. Then went looking for Althea, as usual, he met her in the library studying for her forensic sciences class. He walks up behind her and kisses her on her neck, Althea jumps but was happy to see him. He sits at the table with her; Bill asks her if he could help her study for her class, Althea said yes with a big smile on her face. Then Bill notices Jake outside, standing in front of the library like he is waiting for somebody. About a couple of minutes after, Tracy walks up and hugs him, they were coming into the library, and Bill tells Althea he is going to the bathroom. Jake and Tracy sit at the back of the library; Bill was watching from the bathroom. Seeing Jake sitting there talking with Tracy pisses him off, he wanted to run over there and snap Jake's neck, but that would be a natural death for him. Bill came out of the bathroom and told Althea that he had to go and that he would pass by her later. That night Bill shows up by Althea, she was all excited to see him, and then she quickly went to freshen up herself. When she came back into the room, Bill was sitting by her computer table, and she was surprised.

"Hey, baby, why you are over there and not in the bed."
Said, Althea

"Remember I am here to help you with your work for your forensic class," said Bill

"I thought that was the hint, that we were getting it on," said Althea

"We could do that after baby, "said Bill

Althea pulls up a chair, and both of them begin to go through her book, by the time they were finished. She was dropping asleep; Bill lay next to her until she drops asleep, and then went back into her notes.

Day after day, Bill was over by Althea, helping her with her paper for forensics class, helping her to do research. Bill was learning more about the class than Althea; he was learning what forensics officers would look for at a crime scene. Also, how a murderer gets away without a trace of evidence, Bill ends up doing the paper for Althea. Althea was so excited that she got a ninety-six percent on her paper for the class, and she calls Bill and lets him know. She asks him to come over, he was excited too, and Bill went to the gas station to pick up some drinks before he goes by Althea's. He was standing by the counter, waiting to pay for his stuff. A person walks by him and bumps him hard; Bill falls to the ground, when he looks up, it was one of Jeffery's friends; he looks down at Bill and laughs. The older woman who was standing behind Bill helps him up off the ground. Jeffery's friend asks the cashier for the key to the bathroom, he walks by Bill, and watches him and laughs again.

Bill pays for his stuff and left the store. He went to the car he was driving and pops the trunk. He looks for the tire iron, and pulls it from the trunk, then walks over to the bathroom. Bill notices the person's car parked on the side of the gas station where nobody could see his car. He checks to see if any one of the doors was open, when he pulls on the driver door, it was open. Bill pops the hood for the car and then unscrewed the line that leads to the master cylinder. Then, he went back to his car and sat and waited for the guy to come out; the guy finally came out of the bathroom and jumps into his car. As the guy pulls out, Bill follows behind him. The guy went onto the highway, that's what Bill wanted. Bill was driving slowly behind him when Bill noticed there were no cars in sight. He bumps him in the back, the guy looks in the rearview mirror, but he couldn't see a thing. Bill pulls up next to him, when the guy sees who it was, he starts cussing at Bill, and then Bill sticks up his middle finger. He mashes the gas and speeds away from the guy; he takes off behind Bill, wanting to beat the hell out of him.

There was an unfinished part of the new highway; they had signs at the beginning of the new highway. Bill runs over all the signs; the guy was so upset, he didn't notice the signs on the ground. He was right behind Bill. When Bill saw he was getting close to the unfinished part, he made a quick U-turn so deep, that the tires were squeaking loud. There was smoke in the air from the tires. The guy couldn't see anything. When the smoke finally clears, he realizes he passed Bill on the side of the road. The guy mashes his brakes, to get out and kick Bill's ass, but realizes the car wasn't stopping, when he looked up, he saw the unfinished part of the highway. As he tries to open the door to jump out, it was too late; the car went off the edge. Bill heard the screaming, then heard a big crash, then ran to the edge to see the car had fallen. As he was reaching to the edge, there was a big explosion as the car hit the ground, it bursts out in flames. Bill had a big smile on his face; he went back into his car and drove away.

When Bill reached back to the campus, he went straight by Jeffery's frat house. Everyone was on the porch; they were looking out for their members to come back with the stuff. Bill pulls slowly in front of the house and rolls down the window, and he was laughing so loud that Jeffery could hear him. When Jeffery and his friends look his way, Bill sticks up his middle finger while driving slowly. Some of the members jumped off the porch and started to run after Bill. He speeds away, went left them running after him, Jeffery gets a bad vibe that something happened to their friend.

Bill went over by Althea, when she opens the door and sees him standing there, Althea jumps on him; she begins kissing him. Bill holds her up and starts kissing her back; he walks her over to the bed. When she was on her back, Bill pulls her pants and panties off. As he sticks his head between her legs, Althea's head went back into the pillow. As she bites her lips, Althea puts her hands on his head, pushing his head more between her legs. Bill held her by her thighs and went deeper between her legs; she begins screaming out as her sensation becomes stronger. Althea squeezes Bill's head tighter, and then she releases herself, her body begins shaking. Bill came up on top of her, and then they heard, coming from the side,

"You know that's nasty,"

It was Althea's roommate; she was still in the room. Althea and Bill begin to laugh; the roommate gets up and leaves the room. Bill and Althea continue to have fun for the rest of the night.

 When the morning broke, Bill was feeling great about himself, and Althea was feeling better. Bill takes some of Althea's books with him back to his room; there were from Althea's forensics class. When he reaches back to his room, Jake was still in bed. Bill throws the books on his bed and went to the bathroom, Jake gest up when he heard the bathroom door closed. He sees some books on Bill's bed, and he went closer to his bed to see what it was. When he flips one of the books over and reads the title, his eyes open wide, wondering why Bill had these books, at that same time, Bill walks out of the bathroom,

"Can I help you?" said Bill

"I am sorry, I see you have a new hobby," said Jake

"What is that supposing to mean, the books belong to Althea for her forensics class," said Bill

"Nothing Bill, just that science wasn't your thing in high school," said Jake

Bill walks over and takes the books off his bed, and then puts them on his computer table. Jake went into the bathroom to freshen up; Bill couldn't believe that Jake would go through his stuff. He knows now is not the right time to deal with him. After Jake left the room, Bill goes into the bathroom and takes Jake's toothbrush and passes it between his butt. He freshens himself up and gets ready to go to his first class of the day. As he was walking to his class, he was passing Jeffery's frat house. All of them were on the porch with that sad look on their faces. When Jeffery sees Bill passing the house with that grin on his face, he wanted to rush him and beat him. After Bill passes the house, and Jeffery looks up the road, he sees two police cars drive onto the campus. Everyone that was outside at the time paused for a moment, and no one didn't want to go to class. They wanted to know what happened again. Jeffery and all his friends stand up, looking, and waiting for the news. About half an hour later, the detectives drive up to the Dean's office building, they step out of the car and walk to the Dean's office. After talking with the Dean, the detectives walk towards Jeffery's frat house, Jeffery sees them and gets nervous. When the detectives stop in front of the frat house and ask to speak with Jeffery, the officers pull him on the side and begin to explain that his friend's body was found. His body got burnt to the point that no one could recognize him and that he drove off the new highway. They couldn't understand why he did it, but it didn't have any signs of foul play, Jeffery went back to the guys and told them what the detectives tell him. Tracy was walking toward the frat house when she saw the detectives walking away from the frat house. She quickly ran to Jeffery, when Tracy reaches inside the house, everyone had tears in their eyes. Jeffery was in the corner holding his head, she walked over by him and held him, Jeffery rests his head on her chest and begins to cry.

"Jeffery what's wrong?" asks Tracy

"They found one of my friends, at the bottom of the new highway," said Jeffery

"What the hell? How did that happen," said Tracy?

"I don't know baby, but don't sound like something he would do," said Jeffery

Tracy decided to stay with him for the day; she waited until Jeffery was calm, then calls Jake, she tells him what happened to Jeffery's friend. Jake thinks back on the books that were on Bill's bed. Jake tells Tracy that it didn't add up and tells her to be careful because he had a strong feeling that Bill was involved. When Bill reaches back to his room, he heard Jake on the phone and heard his name called. He knew there was only one person he could be talking too, Bill plays with the doorknob, to let Jake know he was coming in the room. Jake quickly comes off the phone and plays like he was doing work on the computer. Bill just smiled and went into the bathroom, when he came out of the bathroom, Jake was gone. He stands by the window and watches Jake run across the street; he knew it was by Tracy's he was going. It crosses his mind that they found the body in the car by the highway, he smiles to himself.

Tracy was feeling sorry for Jeffery; he didn't want to leave the house, so she decided to stay with him for the day. Losing his cousin and two friends in a short period, Jeffery didn't have an appetite; he didn't feel like doing anything. As the days pass, Jeffery starts to catch himself again, that made Tracy very happy. Jake was trying to put everything together; he noticed that the people who were dying were close to Jeffery; that's what he put together so far. Then it hit him, the night that Bill gets jumped by the movies when he gets out of the hospital, people started dying after that. Jake wanted to tell Tracy, but he didn't have enough proof, so for the next couple of days, he tried following Bill. As the days pass, Althea was the only person Bill was around. One day Althea and Bill were walking towards the lunchroom, there were some students there protesting, they were vegetarians, and they wanted to band meat from the menu, Bill smiles as he passes the protesters. He and Althea sit at a table. Bill notices that Jeffery and his two friends were across from the protesters pointing at them and laughing, Bill knew they were up to no good. After he and Althea finished eating, he tells Althea he had to go and do something, but he would pass by her later. They kissed and went their separate ways.

Jeffery and his friends got up and left. Bill follows behind them; they ended up by the frat house, Jeffery and the guys went downstairs. Bill went around the back by the window for the basement; they were laughing. He overheard that they were going to throw meat at the protesters tomorrow, Bill giggles to himself, he thought it was funny. Jeffery sends one of his friends to the store to buy over a hundred pounds of meat. Bill sneaked back to his room and waited to see when the person comes back from the store. Bill sits by the window patiently; Jake walks into the room and sees him by the window. He finds that strange but blows it off as if it was nothing; he thought that he was looking out for Althea. Bill was getting tired of looking out the window, as he was going to turn away; he heard a car driving up the street. When he looks, it was the person coming back from the store, it was dark by then, and then Bill gets up from the window and goes through the door. The person was offloading the car, it looked like twenty cases of meat, and Bill was in the bushes across the street watching him. Jeffery and the rest of the members of the house came out and helped him carry the meat in the basement. Jeffery takes the last box out of the car, then Bill's phone begins to ring, he quickly turns it off, Jeffery stops and looks around, Bill steps back into the bush more. Jeffery stands there for ten minutes and then went into the house, when Bill looks at his phone, it was Althea calling him. She left a text on his phone for him to come over, Bill waited until the coast was clear then he left.

Althea and Bill were lying on the bed; they just finished her class assignment for her forensics class. Bill was waiting for her to fall asleep, he wanted to go back by Jeffery's house to deal with him, but Althea was talking and talking. He begins to rub her back, and snuggle under her when she begins to feel the warmth of his body; Althea starts dozing off until she went into a deep sleep. Bill slides from under her, and then quietly went out the window. Bill was passing by the gardener's shed; he picks up one of the machetes; he starts to run to Jeffery's house. When he reaches to the frat house, the back door was unlocked; he didn't hear any movement or noise in the house. Bill walked by the kitchen and heard noises coming from the basement. He slowly went down the stairs; he sees that they had a big grinder for the meat; there were some of the boxes on the side. He went behind the boxes that were there, Jeffery and all his friends were there drinking beer. While one of them was grinding the meat, Jeffery stands up and tells the rest of the guys to go upstairs. They leave the one guy to finish grind the meat. Bill stays behind the boxes until Jeffery and the guys went upstairs. The guy was sitting on a stool, just throwing the meat into the meat grinder, Bill waited ten minutes. He walks over to the guy and taps him on the shoulder, when he looks around and sees it was Bill, his eyes open wide. Before he could say anything, Bill swings the machete, cutting his head off. His body hit the floor, and his head rolls over by the steps. Bill walked over and picked up the head. He put it into the meat grinder, and then picks up the body and throws it in the grinder too. Bill stayed and finished grinding up the rest of the meat, packed it in the bags, and then left the house. Bill wipes the machete clean, and then puts it back, then quickly sneaks back into Althea's bed.

Chapter 7
Face To Face

The next morning, when Jeffery awoke, he went downstairs to see if his friend had finished grinding the meat. Everything was packed in bags, but no sign of his friend. Jeffery was happy, he quickly went back upstairs and waked everybody up. Everyone got dressed and went downstairs; the rest of the members were asking for the next person. Jeffery tells them that he went to get something to eat; they quickly pack up the bags. It was still early; it didn't have many people walking around the campus as yet, Jeffery and his friends went through the back of the lunchroom. They went up the stairs onto the roof; Jeffery let them set the bags close to the edge of the roof. Then everyone went to their classes.

Bill was in his first class of the day, waiting patiently for the time to come. He was sitting by the window when he sees Jeffery and his friends walking by; they see him looking through the window. They stick their middle fingers at him. Bill just smiles and shakes his head because he knows what will happen when they open the bags. The time was getting close to lunchtime; Bill left his class earlier, and then Jeffery and his friends went and set themselves up on the roof. Bill sits on a bench across from the building and waits for the show; the protesters were coming one by one. They had their posters and banners in front of the lunchroom, Jeffery and his friends were laughing getting ready to start to throw the meat, as the protesters gather, the crowd was building up too. When all of the protesters were there, they start chanting, "No more meat! No more meat!" Jeffery and his friends stand up and start to throw the meat onto the protesters. The protesters begin to scream out; the meat was falling like rain; one of the girls was screaming to the top of her lungs. Her mouth was open when a piece of meat went into her mouth; everyone who was standing on the side pulls out their phones and begins videotaping. They were laughing; there was so much meat, no matter where they tried to hide, the meat was everywhere. The campus security came trying to help the protesters. The security was bombarded with meat too; everyone else had their phones out, taking pictures and video. Then suddenly, they heard a frightening scream, which made Jeffery and his friends look over the edge to see what was happening. One of the protesters was on the ground, pointing on a piece of meat on the ground. When the campus security went to see what it was, it was three fingers; the security begins to clear everyone from the area. Jeffery was trying to see what was on the ground, and then he heard it was a finger they found on the ground. He turns to his friends and tells them to check the bags. When his friend opens the bag, he drops to his knees and begins to throw up. Jeffery walks over to the bag and opens it, and he sees a pair of eyes watching him. Jeffery starts to shake; his other friends open their bags and find a couple of body parts in each bag. Then one of them tells Jeffery, it's the friend they were looking for this morning, then pulls his shoes out of the bag. One of the protesters looked up on the roof and pointed to the roof, the security looks up and rushes up to the roof, Jeffery drops to his knees. When the security kicks open the door, he sees Jeffery and his friends on the ground, vomiting. Two more security came upon the roof; they handcuff Jeffery and his friends until the police arrived. Jeffery couldn't believe that was his friend in the ground of the bag to pieces, all pieces of his body were all in front of the lunchroom and on the protesters.

When the detectives reach, they see Jeffery, and his friends handcuffed on the side. They walk over to the bags and open it to look. They look at Jeffery and shake their heads. One of them walks over to Jeffery,

"Young man, you know that this doesn't look right, what can you tell me about the person in the bag?" said the detective

"Officer all I can say, that we left him in the basement grinding up the meat last night," said Jeffery

"And none of you guys didn't miss him this morning," said the detective

Jeffery bows his head; for a while, the detective's question Jeffery and his friends, and Jeffery wasn't saying much. After all the questioning, they put Jeffery and his friends in the car and took them down to the station. After they drive off with Jeffery in the car, Bill was on the side, watching them pull off with Jeffery and his friends. Jake was in the room looking out the window; he saw Bill with a big smile on his face as they went with Jeffery and his friends. He knew something was up; Tracy didn't hear of the incident yet. Jake went looking for her, when he finds her, Jake sits her down, Tracy was wondering what was going on. The look on Jake's face, Tracy thought that something was wrong with Bill. When Jake begins to explain to Tracy before he could finish telling her, she pushed him out of the way and went straight for the police station; she was screaming. As she reaches the police station, they already locked up Jeffery and his friends. Tracy was screaming down the place, and she wanted to talk with the detective.

"Hey enough with the noise, what is your problem," said the detective

"You guys lock up my boyfriend for no reason," said Tracy

"And what's his name," said the detective

"Jeffery, you just took him from the college," said Tracy

"Oh, that guy, he is going to be here for a while," said the detective

"Why?" said Tracy

"All of his friends are dying, you do the math, now you leave, or I'll have you arrested for disturbing the peace," said the detective

Tracy couldn't keep calm; one of the female officers had to come out and calm her down. She was shaking; she knew Jeffery was innocent. When she was calm enough, she calls Jake to come and pick her up. Jake borrows one of his friend's cars, on the way to the station he couldn't keep Bill out of his head, didn't trust Bill. When Jake arrived at the station, he sees Tracy on the steps crying her heart out; she gets in the car.

Bill was leaving from Althea's, as he was going to step out of the building, a car pulls up in front of the building. He looks closely; it was Tracy and Jake in the car; he steps back into the building; he also notices that Tracy was crying. Bill was smiling, but at the same time felt sorry for her, Jake came out of the car and went to open the door for her. Jake helps her out of the car, Tracy was crying, so Jake held her trying to comfort her, Bill's eyes turn red. Bill turned around and went back upstairs on Tracy's floor, Jake and Tracy were coming up the stairs, so Bill went and hid around the corner. Jake helps Tracy into her room. Bill begins to punch the wall; he stays there for thirty minutes, and Jake was still in the room. He decided to go back by Althea's; he knocks on the door when Althea sees him, she was excited, she drops the robe she had on to the floor. Bill lifts her and takes her to the bed; he lays her on the bed and puts his head between her legs, but his mind was on Tracy. Althea was in heaven; then Althea pulls him up on the bed, she climbs on top of him, his mind was far-gone. He wasn't paying attention to Althea at that time; all he heard "Bill, Bill" when he looks, his hands were around Althea's neck. When he released her, she jumps off him and runs to the bathroom. She locks the door and sits on the floor of the bathroom, Bill was calling out to her to open the door, and she won't answer him. He heard her crying, and his heart sank, Bill was telling her that he was sorry, he didn't know what came over him, and he blanked out for a little bit. Althea pauses didn't say anything for a couple of minutes, then she opens the door and comes out of the bathroom. Bill quickly gets up and holds her, telling her he's so sorry, he takes her back to the bed, as they lay in the bed, Bill puts his arms around her. After a while, Althea drops asleep. Bill was feeling very bad when she was in her deep sleep; he got up and left the room. As he was walking down the hall, Bill heard someone calling out his name, but he didn't turn around. He heard his name again, he turns around and couldn't believe who it was,

"Hi Bill, hope I am not disturbing you," said Tracy

"NO, you are not, how can I help you," said Bill

"Just needed to talk to someone for a while," said Tracy

"I don't want to get in trouble with your boyfriend," said Bill

"You didn't hear what happened to Jeffery," said Tracy

Tracy asks him if he could follow her out by the tree in the back, but they didn't notice Althea was by her door, watching through the crack of her door. As they were walking down the hall, she was burning up inside. When they reached out by the tree, Tracy rests her head on Bill's shoulder; he automatically puts his arms around her. Tracy begins to explain to Bill what had happened to Jeffery. Bill tries to hold back his smile as he acted surprised, Tracy was crying, and she puts her head on Bill's shoulder again. This time Althea was by the window watching them. She was so upset that she begins to throw stuff around the room; she had tears running down her cheeks because Althea had so much anger in her that she wanted to go downstairs to fight Tracy. Then she started throwing stuff around the room again. Bill and Tracy were there for a couple of hours; Althea didn't move from that window until they had left. Bill reaches back to the room with a big smile on his face, but he didn't forget that he has to kill Jeffery if he gets out. He watched Jake lying in bed and wanted to take the pencil on his desk and stab him to death. Bill was so happy, so he decided to let him live a while longer, he turns over in his bed and goes to sleep with a smile on his face.

 As the days pass, Althea wasn't seeing Bill; he wasn't coming to the study group, she thought that she did something wrong. Althea's worries became anger, so she went looking for Bill, she sees him coming out of the library. Althea tries to stop him, but Bill just blows her off.

Althea stands there in a state of shock, the last thing she remembers, Bill was in her bed a couple of days ago, and everything was fine. She tries to think where she went wrong. Althea walks away in disbelief, another day passes, and Bill didn't come and look for her, she believes that there was another girl in the picture. After a while, Jake noticed that Tracy was blowing him off, never has time to talk, and doesn't hangs out with him by the library anymore. One day he decided to follow her around, he couldn't believe what he was seeing, Bill and Tracy hanging out, when he tries to talk to her she never has time for him. Back at the room, Bill was always in a good mood, and on the phone the whole night. When Jake sees the look on Bill's face, he knows that means he and Tracy are back together again. Jake couldn't take it anymore, the next day he stops Tracy and tells her that they needed to talk, Tracy tries to blow him off. He held her by her arm and then told her with a serious face that they needed to talk. Tracy calls Bill and tells him they would talk later because she had to meet with a friend. Bill didn't like that, but he couldn't show her that, so he decided to go by Althea's and chill until time to see Tracy. When Bill reaches by Althea, she was sitting on the bed with her hands folded. Bill sits next to her and tries to put his arms around her, but she pushes his arms away.

"Hey baby, what's wrong," said Bill

"You know what wrong," said Althea

"Know what!" said Bill

Althea turns to him and tells him she was hearing rumors about him and Tracy, and then she sees it for herself. She wanted to know why he and Tracy were spending so much time together, and she watched him in his eyes. Bill reached over and tries to touch her face, Althea pulls away from him, and he explains to Althea that Tracy and Jake grew up together. Althea didn't want to hear that; she tells him that Tracy has other friends that she could talk too. They argue for hours, to the point Althea broke down and tells him that she loves him. Right then, Bill knows that he had her right where he wanted her, that he could do anything, and she will stay with him.

Jake meets up with Tracy at the library; Jake was trying to understand what was going on between her and Bill. Tracy was explaining how nice Bill has been for the past couple of days, and she appreciates that from him and that he understands that they are just friends, Jake stops her and tells her she has to be careful around him, and she asks why,

"Don't you notice that everybody that gets close to you, they end up dead?" said Jake

"Come on Jake stop talking shit, so he is the one killing everybody on campus," said Tracy

"Yes, I can't prove it now, but just be careful," said Jake

"Jake just stop it, stop that foolishness, he's been our friend, we grew up together, and I don't believe that," said Tracy

Tracy gets up from the table and storms away from the library; Jake tries to stop her. Tracy pulled away from him and went through the door; Jake stands by the door, watching Tracy walk away. He felt scared for her safety. At that same time Bill was walking by the library and saw when Tracy runs out of the library. Bill jumps behind a parked car so that Tracy won't see him. When he looks up by the library door, he sees Jake standing there, calling out to Tracy. He waited until Jake went back to the library and decided to follow Tracy, but he realizes that Tracy was going back to her building. He couldn't risk the chance, he just made up with Althea, and if she sees them together again, it will make matters worse for him. Bill went back to his room when he gets there; he was trying to figure out what went down between Tracy and Jake. A little while after Jake walks into the room. He didn't say much; Jake went by his computer desk; he was worried that Tracy would tell Bill what they spoke about. Bill got up and went into the bathroom, then Jake tries to call Tracy on her phone, but she wasn't picking up. When Bill came out of the bathroom, he lies in his bed watching Jake, which made Jake uneasy, he knew for sure that Tracy told Bill. For the rest of the night, Jake twists and turns. Bill looks at him throughout the night, at one point, Jake opens his eyes and sees Bill watching him, and then he turns his back quickly. Now Bill knew he was guilty of something, and he just smiled. He decided that he would talk with Tracy tomorrow, then try to get it out of her. When the morning came, Jake opens his eyes again and turns around, Bill was gone, and his heart starts to race. He thought that Bill went looking for Tracy; he gets up and rushes out of the room. Jake searches the whole campus for Tracy, but he didn't find her, so he went straight to class. Bill was there, Jake went and sat down, and Bill wasn't saying anything. Jake was twisting back and forth in his seat; he couldn't even concentrate during his class. After the class ended, he got up and walks to the door, when he looks over at Bill, he was watching him with a smile; Jake went looking for Tracy again, still no luck, by the end of the day, Jake went back to his room. When he walks into the room, Bill was already there; Jake jumps back and then walks over by his computer table. Each time he looks up, Bill was watching him, and then he would put his head down quickly. Jake was feeling uneasy now; for an hour, Bill sits there watching him. By this time, he knew without a doubt in his mind, Tracy told him what he told her yesterday, Bill stands up, and started to walk over to Jake, Jake grabs one of the pencils he had on his desk. Bill puts his hand on Jake's shoulder; Jake squeezes the pencil tightly to stab him with it. Bill reaches in his pocket; Jake stands up and pushes him off, Bill pulls two tickets to go to the Lakers game. When Jake sees the tickets, he blew off heavily and then dropped the pencil on the ground.

"Hey, you drop your pencil," said Bill

"Thanks, it was a rough day," said Jake

"For a moment, I thought that you were going to stab me with a pencil; you need to relax, my friend." Said, Bill

Bill was laughing and playing with him in the room; for hours, they talked, and Jake was feeling better. Jake didn't trust him. Still, he decided to go with the flow, for now, to see how far this would go.

As the months pass, Bill's feelings became stronger towards Tracy. One day Tracy and Bill were at the courtyard. When Tracy receives a phone call, she walks away from Bill; he thought it was Jake calling her. Tracy came back with a smile on her face; Bill didn't like the vibes coming from Tracy. She jumps on top of him and thanks him for being there for her; Bill starts to smile, before he could say anything, Tracy tells him that they are releasing Jeffrey from jail, Bill heart sinks and the rage in him begins to rise. Tracy explains that in a couple of weeks, he will be released. For the rest of the day, Tracy was very happy. Bill was going along with her for now, many times, he had to bite his tongue for the next couple of days, and he was pulling away from Tracy. The day finally arrives, Tracy was at the prison waiting on Jeffery, when he walks through the gates, Tracy jumps all over him.

"Tracy I can't breathe," said Jeffery

"I am so sorry, I miss you bad, and I am happy that you are out." Said Tracy

"I miss you too, baby, where is the ride. I am ready to leave this place." Said, Jeffery

Tracy pauses; she didn't think of a ride back, she explains to Jeffery not to get upset, but there's only one person she could call right now. When Tracy mentions Bill's name, Jeffery didn't care, and he was ready to leave from the prison. Tracy calls Bill and tells him she needed him to pick them up from the jail. He was so upset, but he didn't want to disappoint Tracy. Bill went and got his friend's car when he sees Jake walking down the street; he asks Jake to come along with him. Jake knows this wasn't a good idea. Having Bill and Jeffery in the same car, while they were driving, Jake sees the expression on Bill's face. He is hoping that nothing happens when Jeffery gets into the car; they were getting close to the prison, when Bill sees Jeffery, Bill begins grinding his teeth. Jake was shaking when Jeffery was walking toward the car, Tracy had her arms around him. Jeffery knew that would piss off Bill, so he puts his arms around her waist. Bill bites his lips, Jake sees what Jeffery was doing to Bill, he gets out of the car, and hugs Tracy, Jeffery sits in the car, and then Tracy sits next to him in the back. As they start to drive, Bill was watching them through the rearview mirror. A couple times, the car was going over in the next lane. Jake was mashing brakes on his side of the car, Tracy and Jeffery were all over each other, and laughing, Bill grinds his teeth even more. Trying to keep it fresh, Bill turns on the radio to block them out, but each station on the radio was playing a love song, and that irritated him more. When he looks in the rearview mirror again, Jeffery sees him looking and leans over and kisses Tracy. At one point, he runs off the road. Jake had to hold the steering wheel when Bill looked back in the rearview mirror Jeffery was smiling at him while he was rubbing Tracy's breast. Bill mashes down hard on the gas pedal. Jake puts on his seat belt right away, when they arrived on campus, everybody who was in Jeffery's frat house was outside waiting for him. Bill pulls up right in front of them when Jeffery steps out; everyone was cheering. Tracy gets out with him, and she didn't even tell Bill bye, Jake went behind her too. Bill was very upset; he knew that the little time he had with Tracy was gone since Jeffery is back.

Bill went over by Althea to clear his mind; because he was full of anger; he knocks on the door. When Althea sees the sadness in his face, she quickly laid him on the bed; Bill looks up to the ceiling, his mind was far. Althea came and lay next to him; she starts to play with his chest trying to ease his mind and change his mood. Bill won't budge Althea gave up and just held him until she drops asleep. After a while, Bill gets up and goes for a walk, trying to get all this anger out of him. As he was walking, he sees Jeffery standing by a car smoking, and there was a big stick on the ground next to him. Bill picked it up and puts his head down and starts walking slowly to him, as he was close enough to hit him with the stick, out of no way a girl came out of the blue. She jumps on Jeffery, Bill steps back into the dark, and looks at what was going on, he couldn't believe it, the girl was all over him. Jeffery was just laughing, as he opened the car door, Jeffery took the girl into the car that was a parked there with her. This was the perfect opportunity for him to get rid of Jeffrey, but he didn't, Bill stays in the bushes until they were done, Jeffery came out of the car and left the girl. When Jeffery was out of sight, Bill walks slowly to the car; the girl was putting back on her clothes, Bill quietly opens the door. The girl didn't hear the door opening. When she felt the cool breeze hit her body, she looks around, before she could scream, Bill rams the stick right into her mouth. Her blood hits the windshield, Bill pushed and pushed until the stick came out the back of her head. Blood was everywhere in the car. Bill closes the door and wipes his fingerprints off the door and went straight to his room.

Chapter 8
The Break-Up

The next morning, a female student was jogging along with the frat house, when she came up to the car. The student leans on the car, begins to stretch, and catches her breath; she notices that the door was halfway open. When the student looks a little closer into the car, she jumps back and falls to the floor, as the student catches herself, she starts screaming. Jeffery and his friends came running out of the house; they look outside and see the girl on the ground, screaming; they went to see what was wrong with the girl. Jeffery tries to help her off the ground, but she was pointing at the car. Jeffery stands up and looks at the car and realizes that was the car he was in with the girl last night; he takes a deep breath and looks into the car. He couldn't believe it, it was the girl with the stick, sticking out of her mouth and blood all over, Jeffery knew that it would not end well for him. When the word got out about another dead body, the campus security was there within ten to fifteen minutes, and they barricaded the area and called the police.

Jeffery and his friends were on the porch when Tracy heard what was happening. She came as fast as she could to be with Jeffery. It had been a couple of days since Jeffery was out of prison, and she had a bad feeling about this. Jeffery was scared, he didn't want to go back to jail, he knows he is innocent, but everything points to him. When the police car pulls in front of the frat house, and the two detectives came out of the car, Jeffery was shaking. Tracy felt his body shaking and held him tightly, Jeffery puts his head down when the detectives were walking up the steps. The same detective that handled his case before; the detectives see him and smile.

"Well, well, look who we have again," said the detectives

"Officer this doesn't have anything to do with me," said Jeffery

"Are you sure of that, because your friends usually die around you?" said the detective

"Well she is not my friend," said Jeffery

"You sure, maybe your girlfriend," said the other detective

"What the hell kind of question is that, I am his girlfriend!" said Tracy

"Baby calm down, it's just a question," said Jeffery

"Well you need to open your mouth and let them know she wasn't," said Tracy

The detectives had to remove Tracy from the room because she was getting very loud. After the detective's finish with Jeffery and his friends, they went over to the dean's office. The dean put the word out that everybody needed to be careful, and always travel in groups on campus. The news was out; the parents of some of the students came to remove their children out from the college. The police headquarters stationed police on campus to reassure the students and parents that the campus was safe. Twenty-four hours a day, police were on campus, it wasn't easy for the students who decided to stay, Jeffery was getting nervous each time the police drive by their frat house, because he knew that, they were coming back to him because he was the last one who was with her. He wanted to tell Tracy, but he knew it would upset her, and she would leave him. Day after day, it was eating him out from the inside.

After a long day of classes and everybody on guard, Tracy decided to spend the rest of the day with Jeffery. They were on the couch watching TV when there was a knock at the front door; Jeffery's heart begins to race. Jeffery sends one of his friends to check the door,

"Hey Jeff, there is two cops want to talk to you," said the friend

"You need to stop playing," said Jeffery

"Excuse me, Jeffery, can we have a word with you," said the detective

"Sure," said Jeffery

"Where were you between the hours, one and two in the morning? Last week on this day" said the detective

"I went for a walk to catch some air," said Jeffery

"Jeffery why are they questioning you," said Tracy

"They are just doing their job," said Jeffery

"You sure it was just a walk," said the detective

"What kind of question is that?" said Tracy

"Tracy calm down, let them do their job, it was something like that," said Jeffery

"What the hell, what do you mean something like that, I hope you didn't meet up with this bitch who got killed," said Tracy

"Baby calm down, you are getting upset for no reason,"
said Jeffery

"You don't tell me to calm down, answer the dam
question," said Tracy

"Yes, I was with her, but I left her alive," said Jeffery

"Around what time was this Jeffery," said the detective

"It was around 1:45," said Jeffery

"Thank you for your corporation, and another thing, please
don't leave the campus," said the detectives

When the detectives left the house and walked off the
porch, Jeffery turns around to explain to Tracy what had
happened. Tracy stands back and then swings her hand,
slapping the hell out of Jeffery, and then he fell to the floor.
Who were in the house heard the slap and came running
down the stairs, they see Jeffery on the floor holding his
face. Tracy begins kicking him on the floor; Tracy grabs
her bag and storms out of the house? Bill was standing
across the street, he sees when Tracy left the house upset,
and he was laughing to himself. Bill went back to his room;
he had planned to ignore Tracy for the next couple of days.
When she got desperate enough, she would have no choice
but to fall back in love with him. As the days pass, she tries
to get in touch with him many times. Tracy pops up by his
room, and Jake would be the only one there. Tracy tells

Jake to let Bill know to get in touch with her; Bill would be in the shadows watching her every move, many times, Tracy stands there and cries. Bill would feel sorry for her, but would stand firm, Bill knew that she would use Jake to get in touch with him, so he avoided Jake. Bill uses his time away from Tracy to spend with Althea; they would be off-campus a lot, just to avoid Tracy; Althea thought that everything was really good between them.

Jake was worried about Tracy because she couldn't pull herself together; it has been a long time. He decided to go and check on Tracy to see how she was holding up. When he gets over by Tracy, her door was open, and he could hear her crying. Jake pushes the door open, and she was on the bed, crying her heart out because of what Jeffery had done to her, and Bill wasn't there for her. Jake sits on the bed beside her.

"Tracy you need to pull yourself together before you get a nervous breakdown," said Jake

"You heard about the girl they found in the car dead," Said Tracy

"Yes, I heard about her," said Jake

"Well Jeffery was fucking her that same night she got killed," said Tracy

"What the hell, how you know this," said Jake

"The detectives been by him the other day, and he confessed that he was with the girl the same night. But he didn't kill her," said Tracy

"Jeffery just got out of jail, and this doesn't look good for him, but why would he sleep with another girl," said Jake

"I don't know, and I don't care, they should lock his ass up," said Tracy

While they were talking for a moment, Jake thought that Bill had something to do with the girl's deaths. Both of them were on the bed talking; when Jeffery opens the door, and see them on the bed, it didn't look good, it seemed like something was going on with them. Tracy flies off the bed and starts cursing him, Jeffery stands there, and Tracy was hitting him. She was trying to push him out of the room, Jake tries to hold her back, but Tracy pushes him to the ground, Jeffery tries to hold her too. However, she knocks his hands away, everybody in the building heard Tracy, Jeffery felt embarrassed, but he knows it's his fault, Bill was under the tree outside watching all that was going on in Tracy's room. Tracy turns to Jeffery and tells him he needs to leave, Jeffery walks out of the room, and then he turns around to tell Tracy that he was sorry. Tracy slams the door in his face; As Jeffery left the building, and he sees Bill under the tree laughing, he rushes over by Bill.

"You find something funny," said Jeffery

"Yeah, you," said Bill

"You better check yourself, remember what happened at the movies last time," said Jeffery

"That's funny, because last time I checked, all your friends are dying," said Bill

Jeffery paused with his eyes open and didn't have anything to say after that, so he walks away. Bill couldn't decide how he would kill Jeffery, as he turns to walk away, he started to walk behind of him, and then he sees Jake and Tracy coming out of the building. Tracy was resting her head on Jake's shoulder; Bill couldn't deal with it, the fact that Jake would be there to comfort Tracy every time. When he looks back around for Jeffery, he was already gone, this time Jake had pushed him over the edge, Bill left very upset. That night when Jake was leaving from Tracy, going back to his room, out of nowhere, this person jumps out of the bushes. The person begins to beat him up; Jake fell to the ground screaming for his life. The person stamps on him all over. After he runs off into the bushes, Jake crawls to his building; he was in the hallway trying to catch himself to make it to his room. When the campus security came to check the building, he sees Jake on the ground covered in blood, he immediately calls for an assistant. The security calls for an ambulance, word got back to Tracy; she drops everything and rushes over to the building looking for Jake. Tracy calls Bill and tells him what had happened to Jake, the ambulance came and picked Jake up, and Bill stands by the window and is laughing. When the ambulance was off the campus, Bill meets Tracy by the hospital. Bill arrived at the hospital and Tracy is in the waiting room crying. Bill sits by her and puts his arms around her; she rests her head on his chest, the nurse came out and told Bill and Tracy to come in. When they went into the room, Jake was all bandaged up, Tracy sat next to Jake and held his hand, Bill didn't like seeing that. Jake opens his eyes and looks at Tracy, and then he looks up at Bill, he had a smile on his face, and that moment he knew it was Bill that did this to him. When Bill looks at Jake to see if his eyes were open, Jake closes his eyes quickly. At that time, the detectives walk into the room. They ask Tracy and Bill to leave the room, and they question Jake for a couple of hours. When the doctor came into the room and saw how exhausted Jake looked, the doctors chased the detectives out of the room. Tracy and Bill decided that they were going to stay there for the night. When the doctor finished with Jake, Bill and Tracy went into the room, he had fallen asleep, Bill sits down, and Tracy sits next to him, after a while Tracy was getting sleepy. She puts her head in Bill's lap and drops asleep. Bill begins to rub her head and play with her hair, and he was passing his fingers on her lips. Remembering how they were when they were together, for that moment, Bill was at peace with himself, wishing that things go back how it was with them.

When Jeffery heard that Jake got jumped, he rushes over by the hospital to see him; he speaks with the woman by the desk trying to find out which room Jake was in. When he gets there, from the outside, and sees Tracy in Bill's lap, Bill looks up and sees him looking in. He smiles and begins to kiss Tracy on her forehead, and then rubs Tracy's back, Jeffery gets so upset. As he rushes to the room, before he steps into the room, the detectives grab him,

"Hey slow down Jeffery, where you are going in such a rush," said the detective

"I am going to see my friend," said Jeffery

"You sure of that, we need you to come down to the station with us, you save us the trip of going to the college for you," said the detective

"I didn't do anything, wrong officers, "said Jeffery

"Let us be the judge of that," said the detectives

 Bill saw when the detectives grabbed Jeffery; he had eased his way from Tracy and stood by the door. The detectives

take Jeffery by his hand and walk him down the hallway;
Bill watches as they walk Jeffery out of the hospital.
Jeffery was upset, and Bill was laughing, Tracy didn't hear
anything, But Jake was watching him standing by the door.
At the station, Jeffery was trying to explain to them that he
didn't have anything to do with Jake getting jumped. The
detectives watch each other and then watch Jeffery, one of
the detectives starts to read him his rights. Jeffery was kind
of confused, and then when they said that they are arresting
him for the murder of the girl a couple of nights ago, he
starts shouting that he didn't do it, and then they take him
in the back and book him for the murder. Jeffery couldn't
believe this was happening to him again; he was allowed
one phone call, he calls Tracy's phone. She didn't pick, but
he left her a message on her phone to let his frat members
know where he was. After a couple of days had passed,
Jake gets released from the hospital, and he didn't want to
go back to the room with Bill. He didn't feel comfortable
sleeping in the same room. When Jake arrived in the room,
he stands by the door for a while before he enters the room.
When he opens the door, Bill was by his bed, his heart
skips a beat, and Bill gets up and greets him. Jake hesitated
to hug him; Bill was smiling behind his back, Jake went
and lay on his bed, Bill was asking him if he had needed

anything. Jake shakes his head, telling him, no, Bill grabs some stuff and goes through the door. He was relieved that Bill left the room; he calls Tracy to come over to spend some time with him.

The next couple of days Tracy didn't go to her class, she stays with Jake in the room, and Bill didn't want to leave the room either. However, he had class to go to, and Althea was waiting for him. When Bill reaches to his class, Althea noticed he looked a little upset, she hugs him, but he hardly hugs her back. Althea tells him that she would like to go and get something to eat after her last class. Bill didn't answer her, and his mind was far. Tracy was in his room with Jake, and he couldn't stay. Althea taps him on the shoulder. Then asks him again, Bill nod his head, and that was good enough for Althea. During the rest of the day, while Bill was in his classes, he could only think about Tracy in the room with Jake. He didn't want to go with Althea after classes, but he had no choice, he didn't want to upset Althea or let her suspect anything.

Althea took him off the campus to a little dinner so that he could be far away from Tracy. When the food came to the table, Bill picks at his food, and he was looking at his watch and counting the time. Althea notices that he was looking at his watch a lot, so she decided to ask him if they could go to the beach afterward. Bill said no so loud that everybody in the diner looked around, Althea put her head down, and she takes a couple of deep breaths. She gets up and grabs her bag; then she went through the door. Bill gets up and chases her.

"Baby I was wrong," said Bill

"You damn right, you are wrong," said Althea

"Why would you say that?" said Bill

"I have noticed lately that you don't want to be around me, and when you are around me, you upset all the time." said, Althea

"A lot is going on, more than you think," said Bill

"All you have to do, is talk to me, I can help you more than you think," said Althea

"You know you are right, let's go to the beach," said Bill

Tracy was doing everything for Jake trying to keep him as comfortable as possible. She was trying to help him remember something from last night; Jake didn't want to tell Tracy anything, because the person who jumped him was wearing the same cologne as Bill. He knows that Tracy would not believe him, he was waiting to get better to confront Bill, and so he didn't tell anyone that information. It had gotten dark, and Tracy was getting ready to leave, Jake didn't want her to go as yet, because he knew Bill

would be here soon. Jake was afraid to be in the room alone
with him, and he was stalling Tracy, having her feed him
and help him to the bathroom. Jake stays in the bathroom
for a while, until Tracy starts knocking on the door, she
tells him that she has to go, and then Tracy left the room.
Jake was sitting on the toilet thinking on the cologne, and
then he heard the door open, he thought that Tracy had
come back to the room. He calls out to her but didn't hear
an answer, so he calls out again no answer, Jake's heart
begins to beat fast, he waited to listen out for the footsteps.
Then Bill answers, Jake was shaking badly, he flushes the
toilet, and came out of the bathroom and went to lie on his
bed. Bill was standing by his bed. Bill looks over by him
and walks slowly towards Jake; at this point, Jake was
shaking in the bed. Bill sits on the edge of his bed; he bends
down and reaches for something on the floor. Jake's eyes
open wide, when Bill's hands came up, Jake moves his
body close to the wall then Bill puts a wet cloth on his
forehead and wipes it. Bill had a smile on his face; Jake
watches him straight in his face knowing that Bill was
playing with him. When Bill was finished with him, he got
up and went to the bathroom. Jake takes a couple of deep
breaths. When Bill came out, he dries himself and puts on
his cologne, when the scent of the cologne hits Jake's nose,

his eyes open wide, Bill jumps into his bed. Jake sits up against the wall. He was in a lot of pain, but he wasn't closing his eyes tonight. He watches Bill for the rest of the night. Jake wanted to beat Bill in his sleep, but he was in too much pain and didn't have the strength to fight him.

Chapter 9
The Unknown Subject

B ill wakes up, turns over, and sees Jake sitting against the wall; he smiles in his head. He tells Jake morning, and then went to the bathroom; there was a knock at the door, he stops and opens the door. When he opens the door, it was Tracy, she hugs Bill and kisses him on the cheek, and Bill smiles. He went to the bathroom and left Tracy to deal with Jake. Tracy was wondering why Jake was up against the wall. She laid him back down in the bed. Jake had this scared look on his face. He was debating if he should tell Tracy about Bill. Tracy cleans him up and feeds him. When she was finished, Tracy left the room to go to her classes for the day; she was back in her schoolwork. As Tracy left the room, Jake was thinking, so he decided he has to force himself to get better. Jake crawls out of bed; then he fell to the floor. He forces himself back up for the rest of the week; Jake was pushing himself even when he was feeling a lot of pain. Bill would pass through the room and see Jake sweating and wonder what he was doing; Jake would lie in bed and say nothing. As the days pass Jake begins to get better and stronger, Tracy was very impressed by how fast Jake was getting better; Bill notices that Jake started to get better. It bothered him, that meant he and Tracy would be up and down with each other again. When Jake was good enough to go to his classes, he didn't say much to Bill. A couple of times, Tracy was over by Jake, and she realizes that Jake and Bill won't say much to each other. She wanted to ask Jake, but not in front of Bill. One day Tracy was going to her second class and saw Jake in the library, she went in and sat beside him,

"Jake can I ask you a question," said Tracy

"Sure," said Jake

"What's going on with you and Bill?" said Tracy

"Nothing, why you ask," said Jake

"Jake, I know you, and I know Bill, we been friends from kids, I know something is going on between you guys," said Tracy

"If I tell you, you won't believe me," said Jake

"Come on Jake, we are friends, you could tell me anything," said Tracy

"That's what you are saying now, you didn't believe me last time," said Jake

Tracy reassures him that he could tell her, Jake takes a couple deep breaths, pauses and watches her. He starts to explain, Tracy just sits there listening to him, in her head she didn't want to believe what Jake was saying. Jake noticed her expression on her became serious when Jake was finished explaining, Tracy, takes her bag and left. Jake didn't move, because he knows that she didn't believe him. He wasn't going to lose focus on Bill; As the days pass, Jake didn't see Tracy anywhere, he decided not to look for her, to try to explain again. Jake would lie in his bed, watching Bill and Bill would have his back turned to him with his eyes open. The tension was strong in the room, Bill plotting to kill Jake, and Jake not trusting Bill.

A couple of days after, Bill was passing by the frat house and he stops, he couldn't believe it. Jeffery was sitting on the porch, their eyes connected, and Jeffery was smiling, Bill was grinding his teeth, and then he sees the ankle brace on Jeffery's leg. Bill continues walking; he knows that Tracy would feel sorry for him and try to be there for him.

He was passing the library, and Althea was inside. When she sees him walking by, Althea ran out to Bill, she calls out to him, but Bill didn't hear her. He was so upset at the time that he blanks out everything around him. Althea had to chase him down, she saw how upset he was, and she pulls him on the side. She demanded that he tell her what is really going on. Bill watched her in her face. He tells her they would talk when he comes over tonight, as he was walking into his first class, he sees Tracy coming up the hallway, he waves to her. Tracy bows her head and continues walking; he knew something was wrong; he wonders if Jake had told her something. Then Bill begins to think, because Jeffery is back, she is acting differently with him. Now, even more, he wanted to kill Jeffery. During his class, he was thinking about Jake and Jeffery; he wanted to make their death very painful, then it crosses his mind, Jeffery can't leave the frat house. It would be easier for him. After the class, Bill went off the campus to look for someone to purchase a weapon, he decided that he would make it look like a break-in and kill Jeffery and the rest of his friends.

After Tracy's last class, she decided to go back to her room; she just lay on the bed, looking up at the ceiling. She couldn't believe that Bill would do something like that and that he would be capable of killing all of Jeffery's friends. She twists and turns and started to cry because all of it begins to sink in, that all the people she was getting close to, would die. She even went back as far as elementary school, the boy that was found dead in the woods, was her boyfriend, and Bill was always there when she needed him. The next morning, she went over by Jake, when she was walking up to the room, Bill was walking up the hallway. Bill stops and tells Tracy hi and hugs her. But Tracy didn't say anything or hug him back,

"Hey, you ok," said Bill

"Not really," said Tracy

"What's wrong, from yesterday I wave at you, and you just put your head down?" said Bill

"It's just a lot, I am trying to figure out some stuff," said Tracy

Tracy hugs Bill, and then went into the room by Jake; Bill was confused and wanted to know what was going on. Bill shakes his head and left to go by Althea; he forgot that he had to pass by her last night; he knew she was going to be upset. When Jake sees Tracy come into the room, he was surprised; he thought that Tracy didn't want to speak to him anymore. Tracy sits on the bed next to him and rests her head on his shoulder and began to cry. Jake just puts his arms around her; she started to explain to Jake that she thinks he was right about Bill. Jake told her that she has to be very careful around him and to act normal because Jake thinks that if Bill knows something, that will be it. About a couple hours after, Tracy left Jake to go back to her room, when she was passing the frat house, someone was calling out to her; Tracy thought it was one of Jeffery's friends, so she turns around to say hi. She sees it was Jeffery; she couldn't believe it; the word on the campus was that he had to get arrested for the girl's murder.

"Hi Tracy, how you are doing' said Jeffery

"I am fine, I see you are out," said Tracy

"Not really, they have me under house arrest, why don't you come in," said Jeffery

"No, I hope everything works out for you, have a nice day," said Tracy

Tracy continues walking, Jeffery was calling out to her, but Tracy continues walking. Bill was by Althea's, and she was pressuring him to tell her what was going on. Bill knows that he couldn't tell her everything, so he decided to tell her about what Jeffery and his friends did at the movies. Althea was upset and tells Bill that he should have told her before. He explains that he saw him yesterday, and that's why he was upset; he thought that they had locked him up for good.

Althea held Bill's head and rested it between her breasts and tells him that everything will be ok. Bill knows that this would keep Althea off his back for a while; they made love all through the night, after they were finished, he lies there thinking how he would kill Jeffery. The next day Bill went to his classes, as usual; he was counting the hours as they passed; Finally, it begins to get dark, Bill went to his room to freshen up, as he steps in the room, Tracy was there with Jake. Bill walked past them and went into the bathroom. When he came out of the bathroom, he gets dressed to leave the room. Before he left the room, Tracy gets up and hugs him. Bill thinks that Tracy was coming back around again, but that didn't change his mind from killing Jeffery. Bill left the room and went by the bushes across from the frat house, waiting for it to get later in the night. There was campus security driving back and forth; he knew he had to be quick in and out. Jeffery and his friends were on the porch drinking; it starts to get too late; Bill was dropping asleep in the bushes.

One of Jeffery's friends calls him inside and tells him that they had a surprise for him upstairs. Jeffery was laughing, he went upstairs to the room, and the lights were off, he reaches to turn on the light. The person tells him to leave the light off and then tells him to come and lay on the bed.

Jeffery decided to go along with whoever it was. Jeffery lays on the bed, the person came over him, and then ties his hands to the bedposts, and then his legs. When Jeffery felt the heat from the person's crotch, he gets excited, as the person begins grinding on him. Jeffery was breathing heavily, he wanted to caress the person, but he couldn't. The person slides their hand down his pants, and start to rub his private, Jeffery gets very excited. Jeffery was enjoying it, the person puts one of their fingers in his mouth, and he begins sucking on it. Jeffery felt the person putting a piece of cloth in his mouth, Jeffery got more excited. He was grooving with the person; he was all into it; the person pulls a knife from their leg and raises it up in the air. When Jeffery sees the knife, he tries to shake the person off him, and he couldn't scream. Also, the person begins stabbing him repeatedly. The blood was flying everywhere. The person stabs out his two eyes and cuts his throat. When the person was finished, they crawled out the window and left.

Bill couldn't wait anymore; he decided to go back to the room because, in a couple of hours, the sun was coming up. Bill reached back to the room and was shocked that Tracy was still there; he went straight into the bathroom. Bill washes himself off, and then Jake looks at Tracy and knows something was wrong; Bill came out of the bathroom and got ready for bed. Tracy hugs him and then left the room. Jake lay in the bed. Bill lay in the bed and turned his back to Jake and went to sleep. Jake knew something was wrong, so he lay watching Bill for the rest of the night. When the morning came, Jake heard the knocking at the door. Jake opens the door, and sees it was Althea, she tells him morning and rushes past him, then jumps on Bill in the bed. Bill got up with a smile on his face; Althea was kissing him all in his face, and they were playing in the bed. Jake was laughing with them; he was happy to see that between them; he gets up and leaves the room to give them space. Jake was going to class; he was passing the frat house when he heard screaming from inside. Jake runs inside to see what the problem was and to make sure that Jeffery was ok. When he reaches inside, he sees everyone was downstairs, holding their stomach. Jake runs upstairs to see what was wrong, as he enters into the room, he saw Jeffery tied to the bed, covered in blood, you couldn't recognize his face. Jake held his belly and went back down the stairs. The campus security came and told everyone to stay put until the police come; they had Jake and Jeffery's friends in the living room sitting waiting for the police. The word went around the campus until the word gets back to Tracy; she was shaking. Tracy couldn't believe that Jeffery was dead, she went by the frat house. She was standing outside. When the detectives see her outside, they pull her inside and then begin to question her. The detectives knew that Tracy had a motive. When Jake sees that they were questioning Tracy, he rushes over to tell them that she was with him the whole night. They continue to question the rest of their friends. After a while they let Jake and Tracy go, Tracy was crying, she couldn't believe that Jeffery is dead, Jake held her as they walked back to her room. When they were going in the building, Althea and Bill were coming in at the same time. Bill sees Jake-holding Tracy in his arms, and she was crying, Bill stops both of them. However, Althea wasn't happy about that,

"Hey guys what's going on?" said Bill

"What! You didn't hear, that they found Jeffery dead in his bed," said Jake

Bill was shocked but had a little smile on his face; Tracy sees that, and her heart starts to beat fast. Jake tells Bill he is taking her back to her room. When Bill and Althea reach inside her room, Althea tells Bill that it was a good thing that Jeffery got kill; Bill watches her like she was crazy. He couldn't believe that she wanted him dead, Jake and Tracy knew that Bill killed Jeffery.

Nevertheless, they couldn't prove it; they knew it was strange when Bill came into the room last night and also went straight in the shower. Tracy didn't want Jake to go back to the room by himself. Jake reassures her that everything will be all right, and he didn't want Bill to suspect anything, he had to play along for now.

The college closes down the frat house, because of the murder. For the next couple of weeks, not everyone could stop talking about it; again, more parents pull their children out of the college. Even some of the professors left the college too, a lot of attention was on the college for the next couple of days. They stationed more police all over the campus again; the students couldn't walk the campus in the night without getting stopped by police. The tension between Jake and Bill was getting worse, Jake starts to spend more time by Tracy's, and that was getting Bill more upset. He couldn't get close to Tracy. When he would be over by Althea, he was complaining to her about Jake. Bill lay back in the bed and Althea lays next to him, she rubs his back until he goes to sleep.

The next day Tracy and Jake decided to go to the detectives to tell them what they think about Bill. When the morning came, Bill gets up and gets ready by Althea, he didn't want to pass by his room, knowing that Tracy is going to be there. It would make him angry. He left from Althea's and went straight to his first class of the day, while he was walking, he couldn't bear the thought out of his head that someone killed Jeffery. It was bothering him, but he didn't want to tell Althea that would make something else she would be worrying about. Bill was by the window looking out, trying to put it together, the first thing that crosses his mind, that Tracy killed him for cheating on her. Which made him happy, what a couple they could be he thinks, then he knew Tracy didn't have it in her to do that. In the corner of his eyes, he sees through the window that Tracy and Jake are getting into a car. Bill stands up and looks closer out of the window. Then the professor calls out to him a couple of times, Bill sits back down, but his mind was running wild, he twists and turns in class. He waits for the class to finish because Tracy never misses a class like that, which made it suspicious to him.

When Jake and Tracy reach to the station, one of the detectives was by the soda machine. When he sees Jake and Tracy walk into the station, he walks over to them.

"Hey guys, what you are doing here," said the detective

"We need to speak to you about something," said Jake

The detective takes them back to his desk; Jake starts to explain to them what he and Tracy thought. The detective was shocked, so he immediately calls his partner over; both of the detectives take Jake and Tracy to a back room. They didn't want anyone to hear what was going on; they were at the station for three hours; the detectives were intrigued by Bill. They thought if Jake was right, Bill always had a good alibi. By the time they were done it was getting dark. Jake and Tracy were heading back to the college; a couple of police cars passed them full speed. There was shooting by the store just before you reach the college; Jake see all the flashing lights by the store, he pulls over on the side. Jake was trying to find out what had happened; there were some people standing by the side looking in, the police had blocked off the area. Jake asks the person next to him, what had happened, the person tells him, that it was a robbery, but the robber didn't take anything, they just shot up a guy by the beer section. The EMT's were coming out with the body when the hand slips out from under the sheet. Jake immediately recognized the ring on the hand; it was one of Jeffery's friends. He runs back to the car; he didn't say anything at first, Tracy was asking him over and over.

"Jake what happened," said Tracy

"It was a shooting, and someone got killed," said Jake

"Who is the person?" said Tracy

Jake tell her it was Jeffery's friend, Tracy screams out, she couldn't believe that Bill is killing because of her. She tells Jake to drop to her building right away, as they were driving, Jake was thinking, what was the connection with Jeffery's friends and Bill? Tracy wasn't with none of Jeffery's friends. Then it hit him; they were the ones that jumped him by the movie a couple of months back. He drops Tracy off to her building, Tracy tells him to keep far from her, because she didn't want him to get killed because of her. Jake tries to explain to her it would be ok; she slams the car door and runs away. Now Jake was determined to find the underlying cause of it. When Jake reaches the room, Bill was already there; he thought Bill was quick getting from the store to the room. Bill asks him, where he and Tracy went, Jake watches him funny, because he didn't tell anybody that he and Tracy went to the police station. Then he tells Bill they just went to the store and come right back, Bill knows he was lying, and just says that to see his reaction, all Bill did was smile; Jake tells him that he is going to the library and study. Bill wonders why, and he just came to the room; he knows something was up with him and Tracy. Then they heard a knock at the door; Jake thought it was Tracy, and Bill thought it was Althea. However, when Jake opens the door, it was the detectives.

They ask to speak to Bill. Jake let them into the room and leaves with a smile on his face; Bill wanted to know why the officers wanted to talk to him. Bill sits up in the bed; the detective started to ask him about Jeffery; he was puzzled; he thought they wanted to know about the other killings that happened on campus. Bill went along with the detectives, he answers the best way he can, and then they start to ask him about Tracy. His mind was wondering. Where are they going with this? Bill starts to think back if he had left any evidence behind. He knew that he was clean every time and didn't leave a trace; he starts to get frustrated. The detectives see he was getting frustrated, Bill stands up and tells the detectives he is not answering any more questions. As they were leaving the room, they tell Bill, they will be back another time. When they leave the room, Bill sits on the bed, and his mind was running wild, he concluded that Jake set the detectives on him, now he starts to plan to kill Jake before the week is out.

Jake calls Tracy and lets her know that the detectives were over by the room, questioning Bill. Tracy was happy for a moment and started to cry on the phone, Jake had asked her if he could come over, but she says no, Jake begs her. Tracy hangs up the phone; Tracy was crying on the bed, her roommate came into the room, and sees her on the bed crying. She was asking what was wrong with her; Tracy knows she couldn't say anything to her, so she just tells her that she misses Jeffery. Tracy wanted to confront Bill, but she knows it was putting her life on the line. Jake was sitting in front of the pool house when Bill rushes up to him; Bill knocks the book out of Jake's hand,

"What the hell is your problem?" said Jake

"Did you set the officers on me?" said Bill

"What are you talking about?" said Jake

"Don't act stupid, why would they ask me about Jeffery and Tracy?" said Bill

Jake pushes him away and starts to walk away; Bill pushes Jake, and he fell to the ground. Jake gets up and punches him in his face, Bill steps back, and then he punches Jake back in his face, and then he kicks Jake in his stomach, Jake drops to his knees, Bill came over him to kick him again. When Bill gets close enough, Jake punches him in his private parts; Bill drops to the ground. At the same time, the campus security was passing and saw both of them fighting; the person jumps out of the car, then separates both of them. Bill stormed off and went his way, Jake tries to call Tracy, but she wasn't picking up her phone, he decided to go by the library and relax for a little.

Bill storms over by Althea, and opens her door without knocking, he went straight to the bathroom. She went behind him, when she sees the bruises on his face, she gets scared. She sits him down on the bed and runs and gets the first aid box. Althea sits beside him, she begins to wipe his face-off, and she was asking him what happened to him, but Bill didn't want to say anything. He finally decided to tell her what had happened to him. Althea was very upset, and he had to calm her down. Bill already decided he was going to kill Jake tonight while he was sleeping; Althea had finished cleaning him up then she sends him into the shower to wash off. While he was in the bathroom, Althea gets one of her robes out and puts it on the bed. When Bill came out of the bathroom, she puts the robe around him and puts him to lie down, Bill didn't want to stay, but Althea persuades him to stay. Althea had a bottle of wine and, she pours some in a glass for him. Bill had two glasses of wine, and he begins to feel nice and mellow. She slips the robe off him, he was naked in her bed, he was very excited, that put a smile on her face, and then Althea went into the bathroom to freshen up. Bill was lying there waiting for Althea when the door opens, and Althea's roommate walks in. Bill didn't have enough time to cover himself, the roommate sees everything, Althea rushes out of the bathroom and chases her roommate out of the room, she was laughing, and Bill was too. For the next couple of hours, Althea and Bill were making love until both of them drop asleep, Althea opens her eyes. She sees Bill was out cold but didn't want to wake him up, Althea rested her head on his chest and went back to sleep.

Chapter 10
The Broken Heart

He library was locking up, and the woman begins
to chase everyone out of the library. Jake didn't
want to go to his room, Tracy wasn't picking up
her phone, and he didn't want to go over by Tracy to get
chased away. He decided to go back to the room; he knew
that he has to be on guard. Jake reaches to the door for the
building; he takes a deep breath. As he was walking down
the hallway, someone was walking towards him, they had a
hood over the head, and he couldn't see who it was. Jake
braces himself as he was passing the person. However, the
person passes him straight, Jake continues to his room,
when he reaches his room, he puts the key into the door and
takes another deep breath. When he turns the key, Jake

opens the door slowly, and then suddenly someone kicks him through the door, he fell to the floor. He couldn't see who it was because the room was very dark; the only light was from the hallway. The person kicks the door closed and rushes after Jake; the person raises their foot to stomp on Jake. Jake rolls to the side and kicks the person on the floor with him; he couldn't see where the person fell. Jake quickly went to turn on the light; the person grabs him and slams him against the computer desk. Jake drops to his knees trying to catch his breath; the person stands over him. They had the computer in their hand, and then they bash it into his head, Jake went flat on the floor. The back of his head was gushing blood, he had a big gash in it, and the blood was running like water. The person turns him over; Jake was in a daze; he couldn't focus on the face of the person. The person broke off one of the legs for the computer table and then kneels over Jake, the same scent of Bill's cologne, the person has on. He knew right away it was Bill, he could hardly talk, he tries to tell Bill don't do it. The person rams the computer leg in Jake's throat; the blood was running out of Jake's mouth. The person got up and went to turn on the light, and then they take off the hood. With Jake's last breath, he watches the person, he couldn't believe it, and then he dies.

The sunlight came through Althea's window, waking her up and Bill, he had a big smile on his face. Bill was feeling good, and Althea had a big smile on her face. Bill puts on his clothes, and then kisses Althea, then went through the door. Althea's roommate was sitting by the door; when he passes her, she grabs his hand and hands him a folded-up paper. As he reached outside, Bill opens the paper and smiles; it was the roommate's number with her lipstick on it; he looks back at her and winks his eye, the roommate smiles. As he was walking back to his building, Bill was passing Jeffery's frat house and noticed a black ribbon on the porch. A couple of the members was on the porch looking very sad, Bill sticks up his middle finger, and laughs aloud, the guys on the porch started to curse. They were just about to jump off the porch to rush at Bill when the police car was passing by, and Bill laughs. Even more, he passes their building and continues walking. When he was going up the stairs to his room, one of the students of the building stops and asks him if he and Jake were ok.

"Why you ask," said Bill

"I heard the rumbling, last night; it sounded like both of you were fighting," said the student

Bill tells the student it was none of his business and continues walking; he was upset. He thought that Jake had told him something about the fight they had earlier. As he reaches closer to his room, Bill notices that the door wasn't closed all the way, so he pushes the door slowly open because he didn't want Jake to jump him when he opened the door. The room was a wreck, Bill went inside and was looking around then he sees Jake on the floor. He walks over and stands over him; there was the computer table leg sticking out of his throat, Bill smiles, and then he went in the hallway. He calls the campus security; Bill sits in the hallway, waiting for the security to reach. When they finally chase everyone out of the building, they call the police. As the police came, the security takes Bill to the Dean's office for questioning. The word began spreading around the campus that Jake got killed in his room. Tracy was in her bed, feeling depressed about what Bill was doing. She couldn't believe Bill was like that, and then her roommate came rushing into the room.

"Tracy, Tracy, they just found Jake dead in his room," said the roommate

Tracy screams aloud, grabs some clothes, and went running through the door. By the time she gets over there, the police already had the area blocked off; Tracy tries to push through the crowd. As she gets through, she went under the police line and ran to the stretcher where they had Jake's body. Tracy pulls the sheet off of him and held Jake; she was crying couldn't believe it was Jake. The EMTs and the officers had a hard time getting Tracy off Jake. When they finally get her off him, she fell to the ground screaming her heart out. Tracy couldn't stop crying; her mind runs on Bill, then her rage takes over. She starts shouting Bill's name; she wrestles her way from the officers and runs into the crowd. One of the students tells her that they are holding Bill in the Dean's office. Tracy went running to the Dean's office; When she gets there, Althea was standing outside trying to get in. The officers were outside, not letting anybody into the office. Althea sees Tracy coming, and she sees the look on her face, Althea tries to stop her from talking to her, but Tracy pushes Althea out of the way. She fell to the floor. Tracy pushed to pass the officers by the door and went inside; she was shouting Bill's name loudly. One of the detectives came out and stopped her in the hallway,

"Hey, you can't be here, right now," said the detective

"I want to see that punk-ass now," said Tracy

The detective takes her outside and tells her to stay outside; Althea was very upset that Tracy pushed her down. Tracy was pacing back and forth; she was shouting out Bill's name repeatedly, that was getting Althea even more upset.

The detectives sat next to Bill,

"OK Bill, tells us what really happened in the room," said the detective

"Like what, I came to my room and met him like that," said Bill

"You sure you want to stick to that story," said the detective

"What you guys think that I killed him," said Bill

"Well, it looks so, to us, one of the securities tells us that you and Jake fought earlier. Then, Jake ended up dead in the room, and both of you live in the same room. Then, you are the one that found him dead, so tell me again" said the detective

Bill explains to them that he was with his girlfriend for the whole night after the fight. So, one of the detectives went and get Althea and bring her inside; they take her in a separate room from Bill. They question her, and just as Bill said, Althea told them they send her back outside. The detectives decided to take Bill down to the station for more questioning. When they went through the door, Althea was by the door crying for Bill. Bill tells her it is going to be ok; most of the students were there standing watching everything. When they were putting him in the car, Tracy came from nowhere and slapped Bill in his face and spit on him. Althea rushes Tracy and tackles her down to the ground. They were fighting on the ground; everyone had their phones out videotaping. The officers had to pull them apart; Bill tries to tell Tracy he didn't do it. Tracy turns her back and walks off; Bill puts down his head. It hurt him very bad, that Tracy didn't want anything to do with him anymore and that she thinks he killed Jake; Althea sees tears coming out of Bill's eyes for Tracy, and that pisses her off more, Althea was pushing people out of her way while she was leaving.

In the room at the police station, Bill was sitting at the table, one of the detectives sits down on the other side. He had a folder in front of him; Bill was wondering what it was. When he opens the folder, it was pictures of Jeffery and his four friends' bodies; Bill watches the detective and then the pictures.

"What can you tell me about these pictures," said the detective

"That they all are dead," said Bill

"OH, you are a comedian now, let me tell you another joke, why did you kill them," said the detective

"What! You think I killed them, you really telling jokes now, I don't even know them punk asses," said Bill

"That's funny, I thought that Jeffery took Tracy from you, and then he beat your ass the same night," said the detective

Bill slams his hands on the table and stands up in a rage, the detective sits back in his chair. Also, he starts laughing; the next detective sits Bill back in his chair; they start to explain to him that he had the motive to kill Jeffery and his friends, and Jake. Bill was quiet. He didn't say anything after that. The detectives explain that they know about the incident at the movies the time, who had jumped him, and that he had lied to them, saying that he didn't know. Bill's eyes opened wide. However, he still didn't say anything. The detectives tell him about the other students that were close to Tracy that died. They even went back as far as his elementary school days; Bill looks up at the detectives and tells them that he wants an attorney. The detectives watch each other and smile; they send one of the officers to look for the public defender. One of the detectives bends down and whisper into Bill's ear,

"We got you" and then walks out of the room.

The public defender came and demanded that they release Bill, because of the lack of evidence they had. When they released him, Bill went straight to his room, but couldn't get inside the room, because they had it blocked off. It was a crime scene; he wanted to get some of his stuff, but the police didn't want him to remove nothing from the room, because it was evidence. Bill didn't want to stay by Althea's because they would question her, too, so he decided to stay at a motel just outside of the campus.

 He sits in the room, wondering what to do, it seems the detectives knew more than he thought. Nevertheless, what he thought, the only way they could have known, Jake had to have told them. Something came to mind, and then he pauses. However, Jake didn't know anything about none of the killings, and when he heard knocking on the door. He stays quiet for a while, thinking the person would go away, but they knocked again. Bill gets up and pushes the blinds aside a little bit to see who it was. It was Althea standing by the door, he was relieved, and Bill opens the door for her, Althea jumps into his arms and squeezes him tight. Bill was happy to see her, but he didn't want her there.

"Hi baby, I was worried about you," said Althea

"How did you find me here, and you shouldn't be here," said Bill

"My uncle owns this motel, he told me you were here, nothing would keep me from you," said Althea

"Listen, you shouldn't be here, the cops think I killed Jake, and they are trying to pin other murders on me," said Bill

Althea held him by his face and kissed him; she tells him she is here for him no matter what. Bill was happy to hear that; Althea stays there with him for a while. The next day, Bill went back on campus to his classes. When Bill was walking through the campus to get to his first class of the day, everyone was pointing and whispering to themselves; he reaches to his class and sits where he always sits. Everyone who sat by him moves to another area in the classroom. Bill just smiled to himself. Everyone thought he killed Jake. For the rest of the day all his classes were like that. After his last class, Bill went over by Althea's to relax with her. When he was walking through the hallway, everyone who was in the hallway at the time, turned around and went the next way, Bill reaches the room and Althea didn't reach as yet. However, her roommate was there, when she sees Bill walk into the room, she quickly grabs her stuff, and went through the door. Bill sits on the bed and puts his head down. It was getting to him that everybody was treating him like a criminal. Althea walks into the room. She sees the down look on his face; she knows it was hard for him today, so she tries to make him feel good.

After a couple of hours, Bill gets up and starts to put on his clothes, he tells Althea he was going back to the motel. She wanted to go with him, but he tells her she should stay there. Bill went through the door. As he was walking down the hall, Tracy was coming around the corner. She puts her head down and begins to walk fast. Just as she was passing Bill, he held her by her arm, and Tracy turns around so fast and slaps him hard. Althea heard it from inside the room; she quickly jumps off the bed and rushes out in the hallway. She sees Bill holding Tracy by her arm and holding his face; Althea rushes after Tracy, she jumps on Tracy knocking her to the floor. They were rolling and hitting each other. Bill had to jump in between the both of them. They were swinging their hands all over and around Bill, and he pulls Althea off Tracy and pushes her to the side. Then, held Tracy against the wall. Althea was on the floor in shock that Bill pushed her instead of Tracy. Bill reaches down to pick her up off the floor, and Althea hits his hands away and gets up.

"Bill I can't believe you, you push me," said Althea

"Baby is nothing like that, I was trying to part both of you," said Bill

"No because you are a bitch and bitches belong on the ground," said Tracy

"Bill, you are allowing her to talk to me like that," said Althea

Bill didn't answer her right away, Althea slaps him and goes back in her room. Tracy pushes him off her and walks away from him. Bill went and knocked on Althea's door, and she wouldn't answer him. The door opens, and it was the roommate, she tells him he needs to leave, or she would call the police. Bill shakes his head and walks away, he went back to the motel, and he was very upset with himself. The feelings he had for Tracy were gone, and all he wanted to do now is kill her, he paces the room back and forth. He finally realizes that he loves Althea, and he ruined that because of Tracy, that even made him angrier.

Althea was crying; she felt like shit; she still couldn't believe that Bill pushed her. She came to the understanding that Bill would never get over Tracy, Althea picks up the phone and calls Bill. When Bill picked up the phone and heard Althea's voice, he was happy; she tells him to listen. Bill knew this wasn't good, and his heart begins to race. Althea tells him that it was over and hangs up the phone. He tries to call her back, but she didn't pick up, Bill drops to his knees, tears were running from his eyes, and he starts to punch the floor. For days Bill didn't leave the room. Now he was plotting to kill Tracy. She destroyed his heart and his new love, the anger in him wanted her dead in the worst way. He didn't care if he got caught or not. The following day after he went to the campus, Bill follows Tracy all around the campus, trying to figure out where it would be best.

At the police station, one of the groundskeepers walks into the station, looking for the detectives. He sees the one detective that was on the campus for the homicides, he walks up to him and taps him on the shoulder. The groundskeeper explains that he had some information about one of the murders. The detectives take him in the back.

"What do you have to tell us," said the detective

"The night before the rally they a couple of weeks ago, I was across from the frat house that night," said the groundskeeper

"How is this going to help us?" said the detective

"I see that kid come out the back of the frat house that night," said the groundskeeper

"What kid?" said the detective

"The one you went with the other day from the dean's office," said the groundskeeper

The detectives watch each other; for hours, they had the groundskeeper at the station. They finally could place Bill at murder, and that's all they needed to get an arrest warrant for Bill. It had taken them two days to get the warrant ready. As the detectives got the warrant in their hands, they went straight to the college; the dean was going to his office when he sees the detectives pull up. The detectives call him, and they explain to the dean, that they have an arrest warrant for Bill. Also, they needed to know where Bill was at now; the dean went to his office and pulled up Bill's classes. One by one, the detectives went to his classes, but each professor explained, that Bill didn't show for the past four days. They immediately went looking for Althea, hoping she would know where Bill was, and they met Althea in the library studying for one of her classes.

"Hi Althea, that's your name right," said the detective

"Yes, and what do you want with me," said Althea

"We are looking for your boyfriend Bill," said the detective

"You mean ex-boyfriend," said Althea

"Sorry to hear that, do you know where he is right now," said the detective

"You need to check that bitch Tracy, that's all he cares about anywhere," said Althea

The detectives got up and went looking for Tracy, as they step out of the library, Tracy was walking by, and they pull her to the side. Tracy was telling them she doesn't know, and she doesn't care. The detectives tell her to be careful out there. Tracy brushes them off and leaves them there.

Althea sends a text to Bill's phone to let him know the cops are looking for him. When Bill reads the text, he packed a bag and left the room; tonight was going to be the night he kills Tracy. Bill remembers that tonight, Tracy's roommate has late classes, and she would be alone in the room.

Bill parks the car he was driving in the bushes just before the college; he had noticed there were many cops on the campus that night. He dresses in all black so that he could slide through the bushes so that no one could see him. He was in the bushes across from Tracy's building, waiting for her roommate to leave. Every five minutes, a cop would pass in front of Tracy's building; he knows he has to be quick. Finally, the roommate left the building, and Bill starts timing the cops as they pass. When it was the right time, he was about to make his move when a car pulls up in front of the building. Bill went back into the bushes and waited to see who it was in the car; the person never came out. Then he saw Tracy came down and jumps into the car. Bill was upset, and he didn't know what to do now. The car drove off with Tracy; he was in the bushes cursing, and he couldn't move from there for the moment because the cops were still making their rounds. It was two hours after and Bill was frustrated beyond the point. He notices the cops didn't come around for thirty minutes; he is debating if he should move now. When the car with Tracy came back, Tracy gets out and goes upstairs. However, the car didn't move as yet, like the person was waiting for Tracy to come back down, Bill looks around.

Still, there were no cops in sight. Bill lies on his stomach and starts to crawl toward the car. When he reaches by car, he lies on the ground on the driver's side. The person rolls the window down and spits outside; the spit landed in Bill's face, he slowly pulls the knife from his leg and gets up on his knees. The person was rolling the window back up; Bill held the window and swung his hand with the knife, stabbing the person right in the neck. Then he pulls the knife out and stabs the person again, going through their eyes, hitting the top of the car seat. Bill pulls the knife forward, ripping the person's eyes out. The blood splattered on the windshield. When Bill looks at the person's face, he jumps back, and it was Tracy's little sister, he couldn't believe it.

He took a couple of deeper breaths and went upstairs for Tracy; he was feeling bad now. He couldn't believe that he had just killed Tracy's little sister. As he reaches close to her room, he notices her door was slightly open, easy for him to rush in and kill her, and then suddenly, he heard Tracy screaming out his name,

"Bill doesn't do it, Bill stop" screams Tracy

Bill was puzzled, and then it got quiet, he rushes into the room, and he sees Tracy on the floor with a knife sticking out of her chest. Also, when he looks to the side, there was a person dressed in all black with a hood on their head. Bill rushes the person, hitting the person on the floor; they were wrestling on the floor. Bill pulls out his knife, trying to stab the person; the person kicks it out of his hand. Also, kicks Bill in his face, slamming him into the wall, the person picks up his knife and stabs him in his back. Bill screams out when the person looks to stab him again. He held the person's leg and then pulled them to the floor with him, Bill crawls on top of the person. Also, he starts punching them, the person still had the knife in their hand, and the person stabs him in his arm. Bill rolled away and held his arm; the person gets up and stands over him. The person stands on his both arms, Bill was losing a lot of blood, and he was too weak to move. The person squats down and takes off the hood; Bill's eyes open wide; he couldn't believe who it was

"Are you surprised my love?" said Althea

"What the hell are you doing?" said Bill

"You ask me that now, but I told you already, I will do anything for you, and that I can help you more than you think," said Althea

"What the hell is your problem, why did you kill Tracy, what she did to you wasn't right?" said Bill

"She took you away from me, and all you could think about is that bitch, you pushed me on the ground for her, and that's when I knew that she had to die," said Althea

"I am so sorry, I love you, not her, you are the one for me," said Bill

"A little late for that, my love, I killed that little faggot Jake, the first time I beat the shit out of him. Then in the room, he actually thought I was you, and don't forget about Jeffery, that one was easy, and everyone thought it was you" said Althea

The cops started to make the rounds again; one of the cops pulls up behind the car that was parked in front of the building; the cop blew the horn for the person to move the car. The person didn't respond; the cop came out of the car and walked over to the next car. He starts knocking on the window, but the person didn't respond, the cop puts on the flashlight and shines it into the car. The cop jumps back when he sees the girl in the car, with her eyes hanging out; he quickly calls for back up. When the detectives heard the call over the radio, they quickly call the officers and tell them to surround the building. The detectives didn't want them to enter the building until they had reached; they quickly jump into their car and rush over to the campus. Althea sees the flashing blue and red lights by the window; she stabs Bill in his stomach and left the knives there, then she tells him don't move. Althea walks over by the window and peeps outside, she saw all the cop cars, and she smiles, Althea walks back over by Bill.

"This works out perfectly," said Althea

"Althea, I am sorry for everything, but I truly love you, and if you have to kill me. I understand," said Bill

"Nice try Bill, you almost had me, and the cops would come in and see you and Tracy dead. That there was a struggle between both of you, case solved," said Althea

The detectives finally reach; they went to the trunk of the car and put on the bulletproof vests. The detectives send some of the officers to the back, and they take the rest of them with them through the front door. Floor by floor, the detectives and the officers went until they reached Tracy's floor. Althea pulls the knife out of Bill and puts it in Tracy's hands; she pulls Bill close to Tracy. Bill asked her, one question

"How you expect to get out of here," said Bill

"You don't worry about that part," said Althea

Chapter 11

Sweet Revenge

When Althea turns her back to him, and begins to walk away; Bill takes the knife out of Tracy's hands. Also, she slowly crawls behind her. Althea opens the door a little bit because she knows the officers will come in shooting. As she turns back around; Bill shoves the knife in her stomach, Althea puts her hand over her mouth. She didn't want to scream out, Althea stomps on Bill's wound on his stomach, and the detectives heard Bill scream out. They start to approach the room, Althea heard the cops getting closer, and she quickly pulls him back by Tracy. Althea pulls the knife out of her and places it in Tracy's hand again. Then she takes his knife and stabs him a couple times in his chest. Bill was spitting blood; he couldn't scream out. Althea turns off to go and hide because she knew the cops were by the door. Bill held her by her leg, she turns around, and she starts kicking him in his head, but he won't let go. The detectives were on both sides of the door. They push the door open a little, the room was dark, and they couldn't see anything, but they could hear movement in the room. The detective sends for a flashlight.

No matter what Althea did to Bill, she couldn't get him off her; she takes the knife, and she raises the knife in the air; at that time the detective shines the light in the room. He sees the person standing over Bill and sees Tracy on the side; the detective shouts out to the person to drop the knife. Althea didn't answer him; Bill was losing a lot of blood; he tries to reach up to Althea. However, she kicks his hand away, and again the detective told her to drop the knife. Althea looks at Bill with a smile and swings her hand to stab him; the detectives opened fire on her. Shooting her five times in her back, her body drops on top of Bill. Before she dies, Althea tells Bill she loves him. The officers rush into the room, and the detective takes her body off Bill. Then he calls for an ambulance, the detective turns to the person and takes off the hood. The two detectives couldn't believe who it was; they just shake their heads. When the ambulance came, they stabilized Bill and put him in the ambulance. The next EMTs check Tracy's body for a pulse. Her pulse was beating very slowly and immediately they worked on Tracy and put her on the ambulance. The detectives couldn't believe that Tracy was still alive, now they think the case is closed. All the killing that happened on the campus, they blame Althea for it. One of the detectives wasn't fully convinced that all killing was Althea, so they drove behind the ambulance on the way to the hospital.

It had been two weeks, and Bill was still in the ICU, Tracy had recuperated from her injuries. Every night she would go and look for Bill, sits at his bedside, waiting for him to wake up. The detectives would come and check on him; They still have a question to ask him. Then one night, Tracy had her head on his hand, and then she felt him rubbing her hair. She jumps up and squeezes him; she was so excited, the doctors came rushing in. They send Tracy out of the room so that they could tend to him. The hospital called the detectives to let them know Bill was awake. When they arrived at the hospital; Tracy was in the waiting room. The doctors had to move Bill out of ICU and put him in a regular room.

Before Tracy could go in to see him, the detectives went in to see him first. Bill had stories ready for the detectives, they start asking him questions about Althea, and he didn't have much to say. He explains that she was a girl who was in his study group and had liked him a lot.

"Listen, guys, she was good to me, I can't complain," said Bill

"Did you had any idea that she didn't like your friends?" said the Detective

"All I know is that she didn't like Tracy, because I always told her about Tracy, Tracy was my first love," said Bill

"I guess, by then she wanted Tracy out of the way," said the detective

"Yes, just before you guys came into the room, she told me about Jake and Jeffery, that she got rid of them because they had hurt me," said Bill

The detectives were in shock that a nice girl like Althea would snap like that. A couple of things weren't adding up. They ask him about the guy in the pool and the one that overdosed at the party. Bill explained that he didn't have anything to do with those guys.

"But Tracy was very close to the guys," said the detective

"And what does that have to do with me," said Bill

"Let's put it this way, you and Tracy had just broken up, and she started to see other guys. And the funny thing, they all ended up dead after a couple of days," said the detective

"SO, you are saying, that I killed them," said Bill

"Well I know it wasn't Althea because you guys hadn't met as yet," said the detectives

"You are making it sound like I am some crazy ex-boyfriend going around killing all the guys in Tracy's life," said Bill

"You tell me, she came to us a couple of weeks back, concerned about you, that you get upset every time she is with someone. And, that raises a lot of red flags in my book" said the detective

"One thing I could tell you, I love Tracy with all my heart, she was my first girlfriend from my elementary days. But I am not a murderer, "said Bill

"It's funny that you brought that up, she tells us about that too, about her boyfriend. The one they found in the woods, just as you guys had broken up. Strangely, he ends up dead a couple days after she dumps you. By the way, I have a question for you, why were you by Tracy that night and dressed in all black. Also, who kill Tracy's little sister in the car downstairs, because it couldn't have been Althea. She was already in the room," said the detective

Bill shouts aloud that he is not a murderer. Before the detectives leave, they tell him that they had a witness that sees him leaving Jeffery's frat house, the night the guy ended in the meat grinder. Bill's heart was racing; he couldn't believe that someone saw him, and Tracy told them so much. He was too weak to get out of bed, he wanted to look for the person, but he knows the detective didn't have enough to arrest him. Bill tells them that he wanted them to leave; he wasn't feeling good. Also, he presses the button for the nurse; when the nurse came in, she tells the detectives they have to leave. Before they step out of the room, they tell him that they would be watching him. Tracy was still outside waiting to go in and see him; one of the detectives pull her on the side.

"Listen, I need you to be careful around him," said the detective

"I am sorry, I know Bill all my life, I know he is not a murderer, he saved my life from that crazy bitch," said Tracy

"You need to ask the question, why he was by you that night when you came up to your room, Althea was in your room already. So, who killed your little sister in the car downstairs?" said the detective

The detective walks away from her. Tracy had a puzzled look on her face; she sits down. A couple of hours had passed, before she could go in to see Bill, the last thing that the detective had told her was still in her mind. When Bill sees Tracy walk into the room, his face lights up, Tracy hugs and kisses him on his cheek. She sits next to his bed; she couldn't thank him enough for saving her life. She tells him sorry for treating him badly for the past weeks, Bill hugs her and tells her it's okay.

"I can't believe that Jake is dead," said Tracy

"Me too," said Bill

"Althea had Jake believing it was you making all the killing on campus, that's why he was so distanced from you," said Tracy

"I know, I thought she was a good girl, but she was very jealous, I couldn't mention your name around her," said Bill

"And that bitch killed my little sister, she just came to visit me for a little while," said Tracy

"It's crazy how she ripped your sister's eyes out like that; I am so glad that the cop killed her," said, Bill

Tracy's mind had paused for a second. She couldn't remember how they had found her sister in the car. When thinking hard enough, they never told the family how her sister got killed. Her heart was racing. Bill sees the look on her face as if she was scared. Therefore, he asks her if everything was ok. Tracy puts her head on his chest and tells him yes. She stays with him for two hours and tells him she had to go; he asks if she was coming back tomorrow. She tells him yes; she left the hospital and went straight to the police station. She asks to speak to the two detectives; they took her in the back.

"I need to know something," said Tracy

"Anything, just ask," said the detective

"How did my sister get killed?" said Tracy

"Well we really can't say," said the detective

"Please, I need to know, I need some closure, just this once, so I can sleep better "said Tracy

"Ok, ok, we never told anybody about how we found your sister and the only one that would know it is the killer. Her throat was slashed, and her eyes were ripped out, they almost took her head off" said the detectives

Tracy starts crying, the detectives try to comfort her, and Tracy couldn't believe it. It was from Bill. She cries and cries. After a while Tracy pulls herself together and left the police station. She was walking for hours, didn't know what to do if to tell the cops, or handle it herself. Tracy ends up back in her room. Her roommate looks at Tracy, just lying on her bed watching the ceiling. She went over and asked her if she was ok. Tracy remembers that her roommate was studying to be a lab technician. She sits with her roommate and explains everything that happened to her sister, and who had killed her. She could trust her roommate, and she believed that Bill killed all those people. Tracy asks her roommate if she could get her hands on some cyanide poison. The roommate tells her to wait for her, and she will be right back. An hour had passed, and the roommate had returned. She gives her the little bottle of poison and couple of syringes. Tracy takes a couple of breaths, then turns over to her bed. Through the night, she dreams about Bill, seeing him killing her little sister repeatedly. When morning came, Tracy gets dressed, her roommate hugs her and wishes her luck, and Tracy left the room and went straight to the hospital. When she reaches the hospital. She sees the detective's car out front; she knows they came to question him again. She sits down in the lobby waiting for them to leave; she didn't want them to see her. About two hours after the detectives came downstairs and left, Tracy went up the stairs so that no one could see her. When Tracy reached Bill's floor, the nurses weren't by the desk, so she walks into the room. Bill was sleeping; she walks over to him and watches him in his face. All she could see is her sister begging for her life. She took the ivy line and injected the cyanide. Tracy watches him with such anger, and takes the rest of the cyanide, then injected some more into the ivy line and she waited a couple of minutes. When the cyanide hits his veins, his eyes opened wide, and he sees Tracy standing over him; he was reaching for the button to call the nurse. She pulls it away from him; he couldn't believe it. Bill holds his chest as the cyanide was passing through his body. The machine that he was hooked up to begins beeping, Tracy pulls out the machine from the wall, and she stands over him and watches him fight for his life. He was on his last breath, Tracy bends down and whispers in his ears,

"This is for my sister, you son of a bitch, and all the people you killed, so kiss my ass and die." Said Tracy

Then she slipped out and went back down the stairs. She was in the lobby, as she was walking away, she heard over the intercom, a code blue to Bill's room number. She walks up to the counter to signs in to get a see Bill, and the woman by the counter tells her she can't go up to that room right now. They are having a problem with a patient in that room, so Tracy went and sat down and waited for a chance to go up. A half-hour after the two detectives came running to the door, Tracy stops one of them and asks what is going

on. He tells her, he couldn't talk right now, Tracy paces
back and forth waiting for the detectives. It was an hour
after, they came down, and one of them sat down in the
chair next to her,

"How long have you been here," said the detectives

"I just reach to visit Bill, everything ok with Bill," said
Tracy

"Listen, Bill just died a couple of minutes ago; it looks like
his body organs shut down on him. The doctors don't
understand why I guess we have to wait for the autopsy
report" said the detectives

Tracy fell to the floor and started to cry aloud; the
detectives try to calm her down. They manage to get her
back up on the chair; the woman behind the counter
brought her some water. Tracy sits there with her head
down for about fifteen minutes and tells the detectives she
is ok now. Tracy gets up and walks through the hospital
doors, with a smile on her face. The detectives were
confused for a moment; they turned to the woman behind
the counter and asked her how long Tracy was there. The
lady tells them that she had just reached to go up to the
room. The woman said they called for a code blue for that
same room. One of the detectives couldn't put his finger on

it, but the next detective tells him to leave it alone with a smile on his face.

When Tracy got back to her room, her roommate was waiting on her. Tracy didn't get a chance to settle into the room. The roommate came and was asking all sorts of questions, but Tracy just wanted to leave that behind her. For the next couple of days, the roommate was behind her. One night in the room, Tracy was trying to get some classwork done, when she heard a knock at the door, the roommate opens the door. It was the detectives; they ask to speak to Tracy,

"Goodnight, Tracy, sorry to bother you this time of night," said the detective.

"That's ok, how can I help you," said Tracy

"We want to let you know that they found the cause of death with Bill, they found cyanide in his system." Said the detective

"What! How did that happen?" said Tracy

"That's what we are trying to find out," said the detective

The detective's question Tracy for a couple of minutes more. It begins to feel like they suspected Tracy. The roommate was on the side listening and was getting nervous. After the detectives left the room; the roommate was talking nonstop. It was getting under Tracy's skin. She was trying to calm down her roommate, Tracy finally gets her to calm down. The next morning the roommate was afraid to leave her room. Tracy tries to explain to her not to worry; Tracy left her in the room and went to class. By the end of the day, when she reached back to the room, her roommate was still in the same clothes and was smelling bad. Tracy begins to worry that the roommate couldn't keep her mouth closed about it. Through the night when Tracy was trying to study for one of her classes, the roommate came up her,

"Tracy, we need to confess to the police," said the roommate

"What! Are you crazy? They will lock us up!" said Tracy

After what her roommate tells her, she sits there and listens to her talking. Tracy begins to plot to kill her because she didn't want to go to jail. Tracy was waiting for the right time and the right place; then it came to her; the roommate had a car. She tells the roommate that on the weekend, they were going to the police station. The roommate was happy. Tracy is also getting the cyanide for evidence for the police. When the weekend arrived, both of them jumped into the car. On the way to the police station, Tracy asks the roommate to hold the cyanide. When the roommate wasn't looking, Tracy puts some of the cyanide in the syringe. As they pulled up to the stoplight just before the police station, she injected it. The roommate held her arm and looked at Tracy with her eyes wide open and started foaming at the mouth; the light turned green. Tracy pushes her on the passenger side of the car and drives the car into the police station parking lot.

She takes out a paper and pen, Tracy writes on the paper, confessing for the roommate, that Bill had raped her, she takes revenge on him, and she couldn't live with the guilt, so she killed herself. Tracy wipes down the whole car, leaving no fingerprint of hers there. Tracy runs away from the station. It takes the police four days to find her roommate's body in the parking lot. The detectives try to look at the cameras, but they didn't find anything. They were left puzzled about it, but after weeks passed, and Tracy didn't get a visit from the detectives, now her mind was at peace.